LEVINE

LEVINE

DONALD E. WESTLAKE

THE MYSTERIOUS PRESS
NEW YORK

Library of Congress Catalogue Number: 83-63034
ISBN: 0-89296-063-9   Trade Edition
0-89296-064-7   Limited Edition

FIRST EDITION

Designed by Kingsley Parker at the Angelica Design Group Ltd.
Jacket illustration © 1983 by Greg Couch

CONTENTS

INTRODUCTION

In some ways, 1959 was for me a very good year. The preceding fall I'd moved to New York and gotten a job as reader for a literary agent and settled myself down at last to the task of figuring out how to (a) become a writer and (b) make a living at it. In 1959, fired with youth and freshness and enthusiasm, I churned out more work than in any other year of my life, and most of it found a market. When the dust had settled, it turned out I had produced over half a million published words that year (we say nothing of the unpublished words) and had become a freelance writer. In April, with blind optimism, no money, and an extremely pregnant wife, I had quit my literary agency job, and since that date I have never once, I am happy to say, earned an honest dollar in wages.

Among that year's output were forty-six short stories and novelettes, of which twenty-seven were published. (That's about a third of all the short stories I've written over my entire life so far.) One of those pieces, written early in March, was a novelette entitled "Intellectual Motivation" (I hadn't yet completely cracked the problem of titles — still haven't, come to think of it), which was published in the December 1959 issue of *Alfred Hitchcock's Mystery Magazine* under the not-much-better-title, "The Best-Friend Murder." The story contained clear analogies to my own current situation, and when I look back on it from a vantage point (if that's the phrase I want) of twenty-four years I see it contains more than a little self-analysis and self-criticism. I wasn't really aware of all that at the time, of course, or I would have been too self-conscious to write the story. (We do write what we know, whether we know it or not.) What attracted me then — and what I still think is the story's major excuse for existence — was the attitude of the detective toward the idea of death.

In any mystery story, one element is inevitably the detective's attitude toward death, his reaction to the *concept* of death. The amateur detectives, for instance, the whimsical Wimseys and quaint Queens, view death in the shallowest possible way, as a *solvable puzzle*, which is in any event one of the subliminal comforts of the mystery form. Death is stripped of its grief, horror, loss, irrevocability; we are not helpless, there is something we can do. We can *solve* death.

Similarly, it has become the convention that policemen, professional detectives, are *hardened* to death, *immune* to life untimely nipped. "All I want is the facts, ma'am," Jack Webb used to say in his Sergeant Friday persona on *Dragnet;* nothing would make him scream, or cry, or — o'ercome — turn aside his head. (Although they broke with that just once, when the actor who played Friday's partner died. They wrote it in, and on camera Jack Webb — somehow no longer the cop — did cry, was human, faced death squarely.)

But is the policeman not flesh? Doth he not bleed? Hasn't he in his own lifetime buried grandparents, parents? Isn't he aware of his *own* mortality? It was the idea of a cop, a police detective, who was so tensely aware of his own inevitable death that he wound up hating people who took the idea of death frivolously that led me to Abe Levine and "The Best-Friend Murder" *(née* "Intellectual Motivation").

Which doesn't mean I saw a series in it. The other twenty-six published 1959 stories produced no sequels, nor did I ever expect to see Detective Levine again once he'd finished his gavotte with Larry Perkins. But for some reason he stayed in my mind, a worrying painstaking fretful unheroic man, a fifty-three-year-old who seemed to me at the age of twenty-five to be almost a doddering ancient, but who from my present position I realize is in the absolute prime of life. Levine had not entirely explained himself in that first novelette, nor had his relationship with death been completely explored. From time to time I thought about him, and slowly another story idea took rough shape in my mind, but I didn't get around to writing it.

Then a different story took shape instead, a further exploration of Abe Levine and the idea of death. What if he were faced with a potential suicide, someone who wanted to throw away that which Levine found most precious? Would Levine reject him, hate him, turn away from him? Or would he try, desperately, compulsively, to convert the suicide to Levine's own point of view? And if the latter, what would it mean? It was in June of 1960, fifteen months after Levine's birth, that I put him together with that man on the ledge, in a story I titled (sensibly enough, I thought) "Man on a Ledge," but which *Alfred Hitchcock's Mystery Magazine* published in October of 1960 as (and here I think they were wrong) "Come Back, Come Back."

A sequel does not necessarily a series make. Having used Levine twice, it would have been possible then to go directly to that other story I'd thought of, work out the plot details, and have a true series on my hands — if a short one — but still I hesitated, and then six months later, in December of that year, with Christmas coming on, another permutation in the on-going story of Levine and death occurred to me, and I wrote "The Feel of the Trigger."

There are several things to say about "The Feel of the Trigger." First, at last *Alfred Hitchcock's Mystery Magazine,* which published the story in October of 1961, agreed with me on a title; it was published as "The Feel of the Trigger." Second, this story probably shows at its peak the influence of Evan Hunter on my development as a writer. He had run down these same alleys just a few years before me, had worked for the same literary agency, published in the same or similar magazines. His 87th Precinct novels, as by Ed McBain, had started being published just around the time I was first seriously trying to figure out how to be a self-supporting writer. Naturally I read them. They were that rarity, that near-impossibility, something new under the sun, and naturally I was impressed by and influenced by them. I would not for a moment blame Evan Hunter for "The Feel of the Trigger"; I would only say that a kind of specificity of description and a particular method of entering the protagonist's mind did not exist in my stories before I read Evan Hunter.

Sometimes poetic justice is comic; maybe we should call it doggerel justice. At the time "The Feel of the Trigger" was published, an 87th Precinct series was on television; the only story of mine ever bought to be the basis of an episode in a television series was "The Feel of the Trigger." It ran as an *87th Precinct* story on February 26th, 1962, with Meyer Meyer the character who was worried about his heart condition. Unfortunately, I couldn't be home that night, but a friend offered to tape the program for me. Remember, we're talking about 1962, not 1982, and the tape he was talking about was *sound.* He did record the program, and some time later I heard it, and my memory of it is of a lot of footsteps and several doors being opened. Some day I'd like to see that show.

After three stories, there was no longer any question in my

mind that I had a series on my hands, but at that time I had no idea what one did with a series. A story — any story — is *about* several different things, at different levels. It is about its plot, for instance, but only in the worst and most simplistic writers do specific plots repeat themselves often enough to be termed a series. The repetition of characters makes a series, but if the characters in the original story are tied to a theme or a concern or a view of life that colors them and helps to create them, can they live in stories that are irrelevant to that extra element? I don't think so, and I think over the years there have been several series characters who have been less than they might have been because their later adventures never touched upon those thematic elements which had created the character in the first place.

So if I was going to write another story about Abe Levine, it would have to tie in with his relationship with death, his attitude toward death, his virtual romance with death. Death fascinated Levine, it summoned him and yet repelled him; how could I write a story about Abe Levine without that element?

I couldn't. The series might have died aborning right then, three stories in. I still didn't want to write the one for which I'd had that rough idea, and no other story that included both the character and the theme came to the surface of my brain. Goodbye, Abe.

It was, in fact, not quite a year before another story came along that suited the character and the theme; and had the potential as well to broaden both. It marked a real change in the stories, since for the first time Levine was attacked directly in the area of his weakness. He had been attacked before, as any policeman is liable to be attacked, but in "The Sound of Murder" (my title, left unchanged, hallelujah) Levine is attacked in a way specific to Levine, particular to the character *and* particular to the theme. The generational element became more obvious, though it had been there in some way since the first story. "The Sound of Murder" took

Abe Levine farther down the same road, and when I finished it I wondered if I hadn't gone too far, if this most recent experience might not have changed Levine too much, and made him someone no longer relevant to his theme? An odd finish for a character, if true. (That did happen, as a matter of fact, a decade later, to the hero of a series of mystery novels I'd written under the name of Tucker Coe.)

That story, "The Sound of Murder," was written during a strangely sporadic period of my writing life. I had written two mystery novels, *The Mercenaries* and *Killing Time,* published by Random House, and in the summer of 1961 had started a third which I already knew would be called *361,* which is the numerical classification in *Roget's Thesaurus* for "Murder, violent death." Random House did eventually publish the book under that title, with a note in front explaining what the title meant, but they didn't do what I'd wanted, which was to run, in the form of a frontispiece quote, the entire 361 listing from the *Thesaurus.* Read it for yourself some time, and you'll see why I found it striking and wanted to use it.

In any event, *361* was the coldest book I'd tried to write up to that time, a book in which the first-person narrator would never once *state* his emotions, but in which the emotions would have to be implied by the character's physical actions. It was an easy mood to get into, but a hard book to write, and in the middle of it I stopped and switched to another book entirely, one I'd been thinking about for a while, a paperback-style tough guy novel in which the entire world would be like my *361* hero; a world of unstated emotion and hard surfaces. That book was finished in September of 1961, and was published in February of 1963 as *The Hunter* (my title!) by Pocket Books, under the pen name Richard Stark, a name I'd already used for a few of that spate of short stories from 1959.

Having finished *The Hunter,* I should have gone back to finish *361,* but I think I wasn't ready for two emotionless heroes in a row, and that's when the idea for "The Sound of Murder" came bubbling to the surface. Levine is emotional, the Lord knows, and I notice that in this story he even makes a *point* of his being emotional. It was written in October of 1961 and published in *Alfred Hitchcock's Mystery Magazine* in December of 1962. "The Sound of Murder" restored some juice to my brain, some humanity, and made it possible for me to go on and finish *361*.

Another idea for a Levine story had emerged at the same time, fed by the same impulses, another permutation on Levine's reaction to violent death, but that other story had seemed much more of a problem and I'd chosen to ignore it. Not that it would have been a problem to write, but that it might be a problem to publish. The first four Levine stories had all appeared in *Alfred Hitchcock's Mystery Magazine,* but the story I had in mind seemed inappropriate for that market. Unfortunately, I couldn't think of another publication more likely to find it useful, so I turned my back on it, for as long as I could.

Which turned out to be seven months. After four novelettes, after nearly forty thousand words, I had grown to know and to like Abe Levine. The story I had in mind, which I was calling "The Death of a Bum," was somehow the inevitable next step in Levine's narrowing relationship with death. It was not, in the normal sense of the word, a "mystery" story, which was why I knew *Hitchcock's* would have trouble with it. Remove Levine from it and it wasn't a story at all; I had written myself into a terrible corner, the one in which the character himself has become the world in which the story is set. (A simpler and sillier example of this is *Batman.* Somewhere around 1955, the evil activity most pursued by the criminals in *Batman* became the *uncovering of Batman's identity!* If Batman didn't exist, they wouldn't be criminals. In self-referential fiction, I can think of no peer to *Batman.*)

Nevertheless, for seven months I turned my attention to

other things, and it wasn't until May of 1962 that I finally gave in to the inevitable and wrote "The Death of a Bum." It was one of the easiest writing tasks I've ever had; I knew the character somewhat better than I knew myself; I had known the story for more than half a year; I had already decided it was uncommercial, so there was no point trying to please any particular editor or audience. Sometimes writers say that this or that story "wrote itself," which is never true, but "The Death of a Bum" required a lot less midwifing than usual.

As I'd expected, *Alfred Hitchcock's Mystery Magazine* couldn't use the story, though the editor wrote a very nice and sincere letter—not of apology, but of regret, since he too had grown to like Levine. I wrote back explaining that I'd been prepared for the rejection and was neither surprised nor hurt. I then left it to my agent to do what he could.

It took nearly three years, and I don't know how many submissions, but at last "The Death of a Bum" was published, in *Mike Shayne's Mystery Magazine,* in June of 1965. And there the series ended.

It ended for a variety of reasons. One of them, naturally, was the three-year span between the writing of "The Death of a Bum" and its publication; I felt I couldn't write a new story about Abe Levine before the previous story had found a home. This may seem an unnecessary self-restriction, but in my mind the stories had evolved in such a clear step-by-step way, each one leading to the next, that a story written *after* "The Death of a Bum" but published before it or instead of it would at least for me have destroyed the organic reality of the character and his life.

Another reason for the series ending was a change that had taken place in my own career, which had become schizophrenic in the nicest possible way. The tough guy novel I had written under the name of Richard Stark—*The Hunter*—had been liked and bought by an editor at Pocket Books named Bucklyn Moon, a fine man of whom I cannot say too much (but one thing of whom I must say is that I wish he were still with us), who had liked the lead character in that book, Parker, and asked me, "Do you think you could give us two or three books a year about him?" I thought I could. For several years, I did.

At the same time, the writing I was doing under my own name had taken a completely unexpected (by me) turn. Comedy had come in.

Let me make one thing perfectly clear. I was never a comic. All through my life, in grammar school, in high school, in college, I was never the funniest kid in class. I was always, invariably, the funniest kid's best friend. Out of college and in New York and beginning to make my career as a writer, I got to know a couple of funny writers and I was their best audience. I wasn't the guy with the quick line; I was the guy who *loved* the quick line.

Well, I had a relationship with comedy, it seems, which I'd never dealt with or thought about. But comic elements started creeping into my stories in surprising and sometimes alarming ways. Even in "The Sound of Murder," look at how many comic references, comic elements there are in a story which is in no way comic. Undoubtedly that was an unconscious part of my reaction to the coldness and humorlessness of both *The Hunter* and *361*.

It was two and a half years after "The Sound of Murder" before the comic side was at last given its head. In the early spring of 1964 I started a mystery novel, intended to be published under my own name by Random House, about a young man who runs a bar in Brooklyn which is owned by the Mafia. They use it as a tax loss and to launder money, they occasionally use it as a package drop, and the young man has the job of running it because his uncle is connected with the Mob. At the beginning of the story, two mob hitmen enter the bar as the young man is about to close for the night, try to kill him, and miss.

This was intended to be an ordinary innocent-on-the-run

story, in which the innocent can't go to the police because of his uncle's mob connection. The schnook-on-the-run story, as in *The 39 Steps* or Alfred Hitchcock's movie *Saboteur* (in which Robert Cummings played the schnook, and not to be confused with Hitchcock's *Sabotage* in which Sylvia Sidney played the schnook), has certain comic elements built into it, but it needn't be a comic story, nor did I initially see my mob-nephew tale as a comic story.

But something went wrong. The conventions of the form prostrated themselves before me. Something manic glowed in the air, like St. Elmo's fire. Instead of the comic's best friend — *Shazam!* — I became the comic!

I finished that book in May of 1964 and called it *The Dead Nephew*. My editor at Random House — Lee Wright, the best editor I have ever known, though two others come close — hated that title, and I hated every alternative she suggested, and she hated every other title I offered, and finally, exhausted, we leaned on our lances and gasped and agreed to call the thing *The Fugitive Pigeon*. It became the first of a run of comic novels which, so far as I know, has not yet come to an end.

Well, *The Fugitive Pigeon* was published in March of 1965 and "The Death of a Bum" appeared three months later, and by then I was deeply into being a comic novelist. And in those periods when I came to the surface for air I would turn into a coldly emotionless novelist named Richard Stark who wrote about a sumbitch named Parker. And Levine receded.

But he never entirely faded from view. From almost the beginning I had had that rough idea for a Levine story which I'd never written, and which I now realized was the logical story to follow "The Death of a Bum," but the silence had lasted too long, my concentration was elsewhere, and in any event I had just about given up writing short stories and had *certainly* stopped writing novelettes. From that high of forty-six short stories and novelettes in 1959, by 1966 I was down to zero novelettes and only one short story (which was never published). Between 1967 and 1980 I wrote no novelettes at all and only seven short stories, most of which had been commissioned.

Some of Abe Levine's sensibility, if nothing else, came out in a group of five novels I wrote in the late sixties and early seventies, using the pen-name Tucker Coe, about an ex-cop named Mitch Tobin. But Tobin was not Levine, and death was not Tobin's primary topic.

Abe Levine's saga remained incomplete, and I knew it, and it gnawed at me from time to time. Once, in the late seventies, I tried to rework the stories into a novel, intending to plot out that final unwritten story as the last section of the book. (At that time, I thought it was a story about a burglar.) But, although I see an organic connection among the stories, they are certainly not a novel, nor could they be. They are separate self-contained stories, and putting them in novel drag only makes them look embarrassed and foolish. That novelizing project failed of its own futility, and I stopped work on it long before I got to the new material; so the final story remained unwritten.

It might have remained unwritten forever except for Otto Penzler, proprietor of The Mysterious Press. In the spring of 1982 he and I were talking about another project I don't seem to be working on, which is a book about Dickens' *The Mystery of Edwin Drood* (Jasper didn't do it). I told Otto about Levine, about the five stories I'd written and the one I hadn't written, and he asked to read them. Having done so, he then said he would like to publish them as a collection, but they weren't long enough to fill a book. "You'll just have to write the other story," he said.

Well, of course I didn't *have* to write the other story. But the truth was, I wanted to write that story, it had been itching at me for a long, long time, but I had never had the right impetus at the right moment before. Did I have it now? Obviously, since you are holding the book in your hands, I did.

The last story.

I might be able to write just one more story about Levine, but I knew from the beginning that that would be it. I couldn't possibly resurrect the character, dust him off, and run him through an endless series of novelettes, not now. But one story; yes.

There were problems, though, and the very first problem was *time*. The first five stories were all over twenty years old. The final story could not take place twenty years later in Levine's life, even though it was doing so in his author's. Should I rewrite the earlier stories, updating them, moving them through experiences they had never known; Vietnam, Watergate, the Kennedy assassinations, the changing public perceptions of policemen, all the rest of it? Should I rather attempt to write historical fiction, to write the final story as though it were being written in November of 1962 instead of November of 1982?

I've thought about the problem of updating before this, and generally speaking I'm against it. I believe that television has made a deep change in our perception of time — at least of recent time — and that in some way all of the last fifty years exists simultaneously in our heads, some parts in better focus than others. Because of television and its re-runs and its reliance on old movies to fill the unrelenting hours, we all know Alan Ladd better than we would have otherwise. We all understand men in hats and women in shoulderpads, we comprehend both the miniskirt and the new look, automobiles of almost any era are familiar to us, and we are comfortable with the idea of a man making a nickel phone call. Train travel is not foreign to us, even though most Americans today have never in their lives ridden a train. Without our much realizing it — and without the academics yet having discovered it as a thesis topic — we have grown accustomed to adapting ourselves to the *time* of a story's creation as well as to its characters and plot and themes.

Besides which, updating is hardly ever really successful. The assumptions of the moment run deep; removing them from a generation-old story isn't a simple matter of taking the hero out of a Thunderbird and putting him into a Honda. It's root-canal work; the moment of composition runs its traces through the very sentence structure, like gold ore through a mountain.

And if it isn't possible to bring twenty-year-old stories blinking and peering into the light of today as though they were newborn infants, it is equally unlikely for me to *erase* the last twenty years from my own mind and write as though it were 1962 in this room, I am twenty-nine, and most of my children aren't alive yet. If I write a story now, this moment will exist in it, no matter what I try to do.

I have written that final story, called "After I'm Gone." I have as much as possible tried to make it a story without obvious temporal references, neither *then* nor *now*. I have tried to make it a story that could be read in a magazine in 1983 without the reader thinking, "This must be a reprint," and at the same time I've tried to make it flow naturally from the Levine stories that preceded it. No one could succeed completely straddling such a pair of stools; certainly not me. But if I have at least muted my failure and made it not too clamorous, I'll be content.

As for Abe Levine, we are old friends. He's been there all along, inside my head, waiting for the next call. I had no trouble getting to know him again, and it's my fond belief that he is clearly the same person in the last story that he was in the first, however much time may or may not have gone by. I would like to introduce him to you now, and I hope you like him.

DONALD E. WESTLAKE

LEVINE

THE BEST-FRIEND MURDER

Detective Abraham Levine of Brooklyn's Forty-Third Precinct chewed on his pencil and glowered at the report he'd just written. He didn't like it, he didn't like it at all. It just didn't feel right, and the more he thought about it the stronger the feeling became.

Levine was a short and stocky man, baggily-dressed from plain pipe racks. His face was sensitive, topped by salt-and-pepper gray hair chopped short in a military crewcut. At fifty-three, he had twenty-four years of duty on the police force, and was halfway through the heart-attack age range, a fact that had been bothering him for some time now. Every time he was reminded of death, he thought worriedly about the aging heart pumping away inside his chest.

And in his job, the reminders of death came often. Natural death, accidental death, and violent death.

This one was a violent death, and to Levine it felt wrong somewhere. He and his partner, Jack Crawley, had taken the call just after lunch. It was from one of the patrolmen in Prospect Park, a patrolman named Tanner. A man giving his name as Larry Perkins had walked up to Tanner in the park and announced that he had just poisoned his best friend. Tanner went with him, found a dead body in the apartment Perkins had led him to, and called in. Levine and Crawley, having just walked into the station after lunch, were given the call. They turned around and walked back out again.

Crawley drove their car, an unmarked '56 Chevy, while Levine sat beside him and worried about death. At least this would be one of the neat ones. No knives or bombs or broken beer bottles. Just poison, that was all. The victim would look as though he were sleeping, unless it had been one of those poisons causing muscle spasms before death. But it would still be neater than a knife or a bomb or a broken beer bottle, and the victim wouldn't look quite so completely dead.

Crawley drove leisurely, without the siren. He was a big man in his forties, somewhat overweight, square-faced and heavy jowled, and he looked meaner than he actually was. The Chevy tooled up Eighth Avenue, the late spring sun shining on its hood. They were headed for an address on Garfield Place, the block between Eighth Avenue and Prospect Park West. They had to circle the block, because Garfield was a one-way street. That particular block on Garfield Place is a double row of chipped brownstones, the street running down between two rows of high stone stoops, the buildings cut and chopped inside into thousands of apartments, crannies and cubbyholes, niches and box-like caves, where the subway riders sleep at night. The subway to Manhattan is six blocks away, up at Grand Army Plaza, across the way from the main library.

At one P.M. on this Wednesday in late May, the sidewalks were deserted, the buildings had the look of long abandoned dwellings. Only the cars parked along the left side of the street indicated present occupancy.

The number they wanted was in the middle of the block, on the right-hand side. There was no parking allowed on that side, so there was room directly in front of the address for Crawley to stop the Chevy. He flipped the sun visor down, with the official business card showing through the windshield, and followed Levine across the sidewalk and down the two steps to the basement door, under the stoop. The door was propped open with a battered garbage can. Levine and Crawley walked inside. It was dim in there, after the bright sunlight, and it took Levine's eyes a few seconds to get used to the change. Then he made out the figures of two men standing at the other end of the hallway, in front of a closed door. One was the patrolman, Tanner, young, just over six foot, with a square and impersonal face. The other was Larry Perkins.

Levine and Crawley moved down the hallway to the two men waiting for them. In the seven years they had been partners, they had established a division of labor that satisfied them both. Crawley asked the questions, and Levine listened to the answers. Now, Crawley introduced himself to Tanner, who said, "This is Larry Perkins of 294 Fourth Street."

"Body in there?" asked Crawley, pointing at the closed door.

"Yes, sir," said Tanner.

"Let's go inside," said Crawley. "You keep an eye on the pigeon. See he doesn't fly away."

"I've got some stuff to go to the library," said Perkins suddenly. His voice was young and soft.

They stared at him. Crawley said, "It'll keep."

Levine looked at Perkins, trying to get to know him. It was a technique he used, most of it unconsciously. First, he tried to fit Perkins into a type or category, some sort of general stereotype. Then he would look for small and individual ways in which Perkins differed from the general type, and he would probably wind up with a surprisingly complete mental picture, which would also be surprisingly accurate.

The general stereotype was easy. Perkins, in his black wool sweater and belt-in-the-back khakis and scuffed brown loafers without socks, was "arty". What were they calling them this year? They were "hip" last year, but this year they were — "beat." That was it. For a general stereotype, Larry Perkins was a beatnik. The individual differences would show up soon, in Perkins' talk and mannerisms and attitudes.

Crawley said again, "Let's go inside," and the four of them trooped into the room where the corpse lay.

The apartment was one large room, plus a closet-size kitchenette and an even smaller bathroom. A Murphy bed stood open, covered with zebra-striped material. The rest of the furniture consisted of a battered dresser, a couple of armchairs and lamps, and a record player sitting on a table beside a huge stack of long-playing records. Everything except the record player looked faded and worn and secondhand, including the thin maroon rug on the floor and the soiled flower-pattern wallpaper. Two windows looked out on a narrow cement enclosure and the back of another brownstone. It was a sunny day outside, but no sun managed to get down into this room.

In the middle of the room stood a card table, with a typewriter and two stacks of paper on it. Before the card table was a folding chair, and in the chair sat the dead man. He was slumped forward, his arms flung out and crumpling the stacks of paper, his head resting on the typewriter. His face was turned toward the door, and his eyes were closed, his facial muscles relaxed. It had been a peaceful death, at least, and Levine was grateful for that.

Crawley looked at the body, grunted, and turned to Perkins. "Okay," he said. "Tell us about it."

"I put the poison in his beer," said Perkins simply. He didn't talk like a beatnik at any rate. "He asked me to open a can of beer for him. When I poured it into a glass, I put the poison in, too. When he was dead, I went and talked to the patrolman here."

"And that's all there was to it?"

"That's all."

Levine asked, "Why did you kill him?"

Perkins looked over at Levine. "Because he was a pompous ass."

"Look at me," Crawley told him.

Perkins immediately looked away from Levine, but before he did so, Levine caught a flicker of emotion in the boy's eyes, what emotion he couldn't tell. Levine glanced around the room, at the faded furniture and the card table and the body, and at young Perkins, dressed like a beatnik but talking like the politest of polite young men, outwardly calm but hiding some strong emotion inside his eyes. What was it Levine had seen there? Terror? Rage? Or pleading?

"Tell us about this guy." said Crawley, motioning at the body. "His name, where you knew him from, the whole thing."

"His name is Al Gruber. He got out of the Army about eight months ago. He's living on his savings and the GI Bill. I mean, he *was*."

"He was a college student?"

"More or less. He was taking a few courses at Columbia, nights. He wasn't a full-time student."

Crawley said, "What was he, full-time?"

Perkins shrugged. "Not much of anything. A writer. An undiscovered writer. Like me."

Levine asked, "Did he make much money from his writing?"

"None," said Perkins. This time he didn't turn to look at Levine, but kept watching Crawley while he answered. "He got something accepted by one of the quarterlies once," he said, "but I don't think they ever published it. And they don't pay anything anyway."

"So he was broke?" asked Crawley.

"Very broke. I know the feeling well."

"You in the same boat?"

"Same life story completely," said Perkins. He glanced at the body of Al Gruber and said, "Well, almost. I write, too. And I don't get any money for it. And I'm living on the GI Bill and savings and a few home-typing jobs, and going to Columbia nights."

People came into the room then, the medical examiner and the boys from the lab, and Levine and Crawley, bracketing Perkins between them, waited and watched for a while. When they could see that the M.E. had completed his first examination, they left Perkins in Tanner's charge and went over to talk to him.

Crawley, as usual, asked the questions. "Hi, Doc," he said. "What's it look like to you?"

"Pretty straightforward case," said the M.E. "On the surface, anyway. Our man here was poisoned, felt the effects coming on, came to the typewriter to tell us who'd done it to him, and died. A used glass and a small medicine bottle were on the dresser. We'll check them out, but they almost certainly did the job."

"Did he manage to do any typing before he died?" asked Crawley.

The M.E. shook his head. "Not a word. The paper was in the machine kind of crooked, as though he'd been in a hurry, but he just wasn't fast enough."

"He wasted his time," said Crawley. "The guy confessed right away."

"The one over there with the patrolman?"

"Uh huh."

"Seems odd, doesn't it?" said the M.E. "Take the trouble to poison someone, and then run out and confess to the first cop you see."

Crawley shrugged. "You can never figure," he said.

"I'll get the report to you soon's I can," said the M.E.

"Thanks, Doc. Come on, Abe, let's take our pigeon to his nest."

"Okay," said Levine, abstractedly. Already it felt wrong. It had been feeling wrong, vaguely, ever since he'd caught that glimpse of something in Perkins' eyes. And the feeling of wrongness was getting stronger by the minute, without getting any clearer.

They walked back to Tanner and Perkins, and Crawley said, "Okay, Perkins, let's go for a ride."

They walked back to Tanner.

"You're going to book me?" asked Perkins. He sounded oddly eager.

"Just come along," said Crawley. He didn't believe in answering extraneous questions.

"All right," said Perkins. He turned to Tanner. "Would you mind taking my books and records back to the library? They're due today. They're the ones on that chair. And there's a couple more over in the stack of Al's records."

"Sure," said Tanner. He was gazing at Perkins with a troubled look on his face, and Levine wondered if Tanner felt the same wrongness that was plaguing him.

"Let's go," said Crawley impatiently, and Perkins moved toward the door.

"I'll be right along," said Levine. As Crawley and Perkins left the apartment, Levine glanced at the titles of the books and record albums Perkins had wanted returned to the library. Two of the books were collections of Elizabethan plays, one was the New Arts Writing Annual, and the other two were books on criminology. The records were mainly folk songs, of the bloodier type.

Levine frowned and went over to Tanner. He asked, "What were you and Perkins talking about before we got here?"

Tanner's face was still creased in a puzzled frown. "The stupidity of the criminal mind," he said. "There's something goofy here, Lieutenant."

"You may be right," Levine told him. He walked on down the hall and joined the other two at the door.

All three got into the front seat of the Chevy, Crawley driving again and Perkins sitting in the middle. They rode in silence, Crawley busy driving, Perkins studying the complex array of the dashboard, with its extra knobs and switches and the mike hooked beneath the radio, and Levine trying to figure out what was wrong.

At the station, after booking, they brought him to a small office, one of the interrogation rooms. There was a bare and battered desk, plus four chairs. Crawley sat behind the desk, Perkins sat across the desk and facing him, Levine took the chair in a corner behind and to the left of Perkins, and a male stenographer, notebook in hand, filled the fourth chair, behind Crawley.

Crawley's first questions covered the same ground already covered at Gruber's apartment, this time for the record. "Okay," said Crawley, when he'd brought them up to date. "You and Gruber were both doing the same kind of thing, living the same kind of life. You were both unpublished writers, both taking night courses at Columbia, both living on very little money."

"That's right," said Perkins.

"How long you known each other?"

"About six months. We met at Columbia, and we took the same subway home after class. We got to talking, found out we were both dreaming the same kind of dream, and became friends. You know. Misery loves company."

"Take the same classes at Columbia?"

"Only one. Creative Writing, from Professor Stonegell."

"Where'd you buy the poison?"

"I didn't. Al did. He bought it a while back and just kept it around. He kept saying if he didn't make a good sale soon he'd kill himself. But he didn't mean it. It was just a kind of gag."

Crawley pulled at his right earlobe. Levine knew, from his long experience with his partner, that that gesture meant that Crawley was confused. "You went there today to kill him?"

"That's right."

Levine shook his head. That wasn't right. Softly, he said, "Why did you bring the library books along?"

"I was on my way up to the library," said Perkins, twisting around in his seat to look at Levine.

"Look this way," snapped Crawley.

Perkins looked around at Crawley again, but not before Levine had seen that same burning deep in Perkins' eyes. Stronger, this time, and more like pleading. Pleading? What was Perkins pleading for?

"I was on my way to the library," Perkins said again. "Al had a couple of records out on my card, so I went over to get them. On the way, I decided to kill him."

"Why?" asked Crawley.

"Because he was a pompous ass," said Perkins, the same answer he'd given before.

"Because he got a story accepted by one of the literary magazines and you didn't?" suggested Crawley.

"Maybe. Partially. His whole attitude. He was smug. He knew more than anybody else in the world."

"Why did you kill him today? Why not last week or next week?"

"I felt like it today."

"Why did you give yourself up?"

"You would have gotten me anyway."

Levine asked, "Did you know that before you killed him?"

"I don't know," said Perkins, without looking around at Levine. "I didn't think about it till afterward. Then I knew the police would get me anyway—they'd talk to Professor Stonegell and the other people who knew us both and I didn't want to have to wait it out. So I went and confessed."

"You told the policeman," said Levine, "that you'd killed your best friend."

"That's right."

"Why did you use that phrase, best friend, if you hated him so much you wanted to kill him?"

"He was my best friend. At least, in New York. I didn't really know anyone else, except Professor Stonegell. Al was my best friend because he was just about my only friend."

"Are you sorry you killed him?" asked Levine.

This time, Perkins twisted around in the chair again, ignoring Crawley. "No, sir," he said, and his eyes now were blank.

There was silence in the room, and Crawley and Levine looked at one another. Crawley questioned with his eyes, and Levine shrugged, shaking his head. Something was wrong, but he didn't know what. And Perkins was being so helpful that he wound up being no help at all.

Crawley turned to the stenographer. "Type it up formal," he said. "And have somebody come take the pigeon to his nest."

After the stenographer had left, Levine said, "Anything you want to say off the record, Perkins?"

Perkins grinned. His face was half-turned away from Crawley, and he was looking at the floor, as though he was amused by something he saw there. "Off the record?" he murmured. "As long as there are two of you in here, it's *on* the record."

"Do you want one of us to leave?"

Perkins looked up at Levine again, and stopped smiling. He seemed to think it over for a minute, and then he shook his head. "No," he said. "Thanks, anyway. But I don't think I have anything more to say. Not right now anyway."

Levine frowned and sat back in his chair, studying Perkins. The boy didn't ring true; he was constructed of too many contradictions. Levine reached out for a mental image of Perkins, but all he touched was air.

After Perkins was led out of the room by two uniformed cops, Crawley got to his feet, stretched, sighed, scratched, pulled his earlobe, and said, "What do you make of it, Abe?"

"I don't like it."

"I know that. I saw it in your face. But he confessed, so what else is there?"

"The phony confession is not exactly unheard of, you know."

"Not this time," said Crawley. "A guy confesses to a crime he didn't commit for one of two reasons. Either he's a crackpot who wants the publicity or to be punished or something like that, or he's protecting somebody else. Perkins doesn't read like a crackpot to me, and there's nobody else involved for him to be protecting."

"In a capital punishment state," suggested Levine, "a guy might confess to a murder he didn't commit so the state would do his suicide for him."

Crawley shook his head. "That still doesn't look like Perkins," he said.

"Nothing looks like Perkins. He's given us a blank wall to stare at. A couple of times it started to slip, and there was something else inside."

"Don't build a big thing, Abe. The kid confessed. He's the killer; let it go at that."

"The job's finished, I know that. But it still bothers me."

"Okay," said Crawley. He sat down behind the desk again and put his feet up on the scarred desk top. "Let's straighten it out. Where does it bother you?"

"All over. Number one, motivation. You don't kill a man for being a pompous ass. Not when you turn around a minute later and say he was your best friend."

"People do funny things when they're pushed far enough. Even to friends."

"Sure. Okay, number two. The murder method. It doesn't sound right. When a man kills impulsively, he grabs something and starts swinging. When he calms down, he goes and turns himself in. But when you *poison* somebody, you're using a pretty sneaky method. It doesn't make sense for you to run out and call a cop right after using poison. It isn't the same kind of mentality."

"He used the poison," said Crawley, "because it was handy. Gruber bought it, probably had it sitting on his dresser or something, and Perkins just picked it up on impulse and poured it into the beer."

"That's another thing," said Levine. "Do you drink much beer out of cans?"

Crawley grinned. "You know I do."

"I saw some empty beer cans sitting around the apartment, so that's where Gruber got his last beer from."

"Yeah. So what?"

"When you drink a can of beer, do you pour the beer out of the can into a glass, or do you just drink it straight from the can?"

"I drink it out of the can. But not everybody does."

"I know, I know. Okay, what about the library books? If you're going to kill somebody, are you going to bring library books along?"

"It was an impulse killing. He didn't know he was going to do it until he got there."

Levine got his feet. "That's the hell of it," he said. "You can explain away every single question in this business. But it's such a simple case. Why should there be so many questions that need explaining away?"

Crawley shrugged. "Beats me," he said. "All I know is, we've got a confession, and that's enough to satisfy me."

"Not me," said Levine. "I think I'll go poke around and see what happens. Want to come along?"

"Somebody's going to have to hand the pen to Perkins when he signs his confession," said Crawley.

"Mind if I take off for a while?"

"Go ahead. Have a big time," said Crawley, grinning at him. "Play detective."

Levine's first stop was back at Gruber's address. Gruber's apartment was empty now, having been sifted completely through normal routine procedure. Levine went down to the basement door under the stoop, but he didn't go back to Gruber's door. He stopped at the front apartment instead, where a ragged-edged strip of paper attached with peeling scotch tape to the door read, in awkward and childish lettering, SUPERINTENDENT. Levine rapped and waited. After a minute, the door opened a couple of inches, held by a chain. A round face peered out at him from a height of a little over five feet. The face said, "Who you looking for?"

"Police," Levine told him. He opened his wallet and held it up for the face to look at.

"Oh," said the face. "Sure thing." The door shut, and Levine waited while the chain was clinked free, and then the door opened wide.

The super was a short and round man, dressed in corduroy trousers and a grease-spotted undershirt. He wheezed, "Come in, come in," and stood back for Levine to come into his crowded and musty-smelling living room.

Levine said, "I want to talk to you about Al Gruber."

The super shut the door and waddled into the middle of the room, shaking his head. "Wasn't that a shame?" he asked. "Al was a nice boy. No money, but a nice boy. Sit down somewhere, anywhere."

Levine looked around. The room was full of low-slung, heavy, sagging, over-stuffed furniture, armchairs and sofas. He picked the least battered armchair of the lot, and sat on the very edge. Although he was a short man, his knees seemed to be almost up to his chin, and he had the feeling that if he relaxed he'd fall over backwards.

The super trundled across the room and dropped into one of the other armchairs, sinking into it as though he never intended to get to his feet again in his life. "A real shame," he said again. "And to think I maybe could have stopped it."

"You could have stopped it? How?"

"It was around noon," said the super. "I was watching the TV over there, and I heard a voice from the back apartment, shouting, 'Al! Al!' So I went out to the hall, but by the time I got there the shouting was all done. So I didn't know what to do. I waited a minute, and then I came back in and watched the TV again. That was probably when it was happening."

"There wasn't any noise while you were in the hall? Just the two shouts before you got out there?"

"That's all. At first, I thought it was another one of them arguments, and I was gonna bawl out the two of them, but it stopped before I even got the door open."

"Arguments?"

"Mr. Gruber and Mr. Perkins. They used to argue all the time, shout at each other, carry on like monkeys. The other tenants was always complaining about it. They'd do it late at night sometimes, two or three o'clock in the morning, and the tenants would all start phoning me to complain."

"What did they argue about?"

The super shrugged his massive shoulders. "Who knows? Names. People. Writers. They both think they're great writers or something."

"Did they ever get into a fist fight or anything like that? Ever threaten to kill each other?"

"Naw, they'd just shout at each other and call each other stupid and ignorant and stuff like that. They liked each other, really, I guess. At least they always hung around together. They just loved to argue, that's all. You know how it is with college kids. I've had college kids renting here before, and they're all like that. They all love to argue. Course, I never had nothing like this happen before."

"What kind of person was Gruber, exactly?"

The super mulled it over for a while. "Kind of a quiet guy," he said at last. "Except when he was with Mr. Perkins, I mean. Then he'd shout just as loud and often as anybody. But most of the time he was quiet. And good-mannered. A real surprise, after most of the kids around today. He was always polite, and he'd lend a hand if you needed some help or something, like the time I was carrying a bed up to the third floor front. Mr. Gruber come along and pitched right in with me. He did more of the work than I did."

"And he was a writer, wasn't he? At least, he was trying to be a writer."

"Oh, sure. I'd hear that typewriter of his tappin' away in there at all hours. And he always carried a notebook around with him, writin' things down in it. I asked him once what he wrote in there, and he said descriptions, of places like Prospect Park up at the corner, and of the people he knew. He always said he wanted to be a writer like some guy named Wolfe, used to live in Brooklyn too."

"I see." Levine struggled out of the armchair. "Thanks for your time," he said.

"Not at all." The super waddled after Levine to the door. "Anything I can do," he said. "Any time at all."

"Thanks again," said Levine. He went outside and stood in the hallway, thinking things over, listening to the latch click in place behind him. Then he turned and walked down the hallway to Gruber's apartment, and knocked on the door.

As he'd expected, a uniformed cop had been left behind to keep an eye on the place for a while, and when he opened the door, Levine showed his identification and said, "I'm on the case. I'd like to take a look around."

The cop let him in, and Levine looked carefully through Gruber's personal property. He found the notebooks, finally, in the bottom drawer of the dresser. There were five of them, steno pad size loose-leaf fillers. Four of them were filled with writing, in pen, in a slow and careful hand, and the fifth was still half blank.

Levine carried the notebooks over to the card table, pushed the typewriter out of the way, sat down and began to skim through the books.

He found what he was looking for in the middle of the third one he tried. A description of Larry Perkins, written by the man Perkins had killed. The description, or character study, which it more closely resembled, was four pages long, beginning with a physical description and moving into a discussion of Perkins' personality. Levine noticed particular sentences in this latter part: "Larry doesn't want to write, he wants to be a writer, and that isn't the same thing. He wants the glamour and the fame and the money, and he thinks he'll get it from being a writer. That's why he's dabbled in acting and painting and all the other so-called glamorous professions. Larry and I are both being thwarted by the same thing: neither of us has anything to say worth saying. The difference is, I'm trying to find something to say, and Larry wants to make it on glibness alone. One of these days, he's going to find out he won't get anywhere that way. That's going to be a terrible day for him."

Levine closed the book, then picked up the last one, the one that hadn't yet been filled, and leafed through that. One word kept showing up throughout the last notebook. "Nihilism." Gruber obviously hated the word, and he was also obviously afraid of it. "Nihilism is death," he wrote on one page. "It is the belief that there are no beliefs, that no effort is worthwhile. How could any writer believe such a thing? Writing is the most positive of acts. So how can it be used for negative purposes? The only expression of nihilism is death, not the written word. If I can say nothing hopeful, I shouldn't say anything at all."

Levine put the notebooks back in the dresser drawer finally, thanked the cop, and went out to the Chevy. He'd hoped to be able to fill in the blank spaces in Perkins' character through Gruber's notebooks, but Gruber had apparently had just as much trouble defining Perkins as Levine was now having. Levine had learned a lot about the dead man, that he was sincere and intense and self-demanding as only the young can be, but Perkins was still little more than a smooth and blank wall. "Glibness," Gruber had called it. What was beneath the glibness? A murderer, by Perkins' own admission. But what else?

Levine crawled wearily into the Chevy and headed for Manhattan.

Professor Harvey Stonegell was in class when Levine got to Columbia University, but the girl at the desk in the dean's outer office told him that Stonegell would be out of that class in just a few minutes, and would then be free for the rest of the afternoon. She gave him directions to Stonegell's office, and Levine thanked her.

Stonegell's office door was locked, so Levine waited in the hall, watching students hurrying by in both directions, and reading the notices of scholarships, grants and fellowships thumbtacked to the bulletin board near the office door.

The professor showed up about fifteen minutes later, with two students in tow. He was a tall and slender man, with a gaunt face and a full head of gray-white hair. He could have been any age between fifty and seventy. He wore a tweed suit jacket, leather patches at the elbows, and non-matching gray slacks.

Levine said, "Professor Stonegell?"

"Yes?"

Levine introduced himself and showed his identification. "I'd like to talk to you for a minute or two."

"Of course. I'll just be a minute." Stonegell handed a book to one of the two students, telling him to read certain sections of it, and explained to the other student why he hadn't received a passing grade in his latest assignment. When both of them were taken care of, Levine stepped into Stonegell's crowded and tiny office, and sat down in the chair beside the desk.

Stonegell said, "Is this about one of my students?"

"Two of them. From your evening writing course. Gruber and Perkins."

"Those two? They aren't in trouble, are they?"

"I'm afraid so. Perkins has confessed to murdering Gruber."

Stonegell's thin face paled. "Gruber's dead? Murdered?"

"By Perkins. He turned himself in right after it happened. But, to be honest with you, the whole thing bothers me. It doesn't make sense. You knew them both. I thought you might be able to tell me something about them, so it *would* make sense."

Stonegell lit himself a cigarette and offered one to Levine. Then he fussed rather vaguely with his messy desktop, while Levine waited for him to gather his thoughts.

"This takes some getting used to," said Stonegell after a minute. "Gruber and Perkins. They were both good students in my class, Gruber perhaps a bit better. And they were friends."

"I'd heard they were friends."

"There was a friendly rivalry between them," said Stonegell. "Whenever one of them started a project, the other one started a similar project, intent on beating the first one at his own game. Actually, that was more Perkins than Gruber. And they always took opposite sides of every question, screamed at each other like sworn enemies. But actually they were very close friends. I can't understand either one of them murdering the other."

"Was Gruber similar to Perkins?"

"Did I give that impression? No, they were definitely unalike. The old business about opposites attracting. Gruber was by far the more sensitive and sincere of the two. I don't mean to imply that Perkins was insensitive or insincere at all. Perkins had his own sensitivity and his own sincerity, but they were almost exclusively directed within himself. He equated everything with himself, his own feelings and his own ambitions. But Gruber had more of the — oh, I don't know — more of a *world-view*, to badly translate the German. His sensitivity was directed outward, toward the feelings of other people. It showed up in their writing. Gruber's forté was characterization, subtle interplay between personalities. Perkins was deft, almost glib, with movement and action and plot, but his characters lacked substance. He wasn't really interested in anyone but himself."

"He doesn't sound like the kind of guy who'd confess to a murder right after he committed it."

"I know what you mean. That isn't like him. I don't imagine Perkins would ever feel remorse or guilt. I should think he would be one of the people who believes the only crime is in being caught."

"Yet we didn't catch him. He came to us." Levine studied the book titles on the shelf behind Stonegell. "What about their mental attitudes recently?" he asked. "Generally speaking, I mean. Were they happy or unhappy, impatient or content or what?"

"I think they were both rather depressed, actually," said Stonegell. "Though for somewhat different reasons. They had both come out of the Army less than a year ago, and had come to New York to try to make their mark as writers. Gruber was having difficulty with subject matter. We talked about it a few times. He couldn't find anything he really wanted to write about, nothing he felt strongly enough to give him direction in his writing."

"And Perkins?"

"He wasn't particularly worried about writing in that way. He was, as I say, deft and clever in his writing, but it was all too shallow. I think they might have been bad for one another, actually. Perkins could see that Gruber had the depth and sincerity that he lacked, and Gruber thought that Perkins was free from the soul-searching and self-doubt that was hampering him so much. In the last month or so, both of them have talked about dropping out of school, going back home and forgetting about the whole thing. But neither of them could have done that, at least not yet. Gruber couldn't have, because the desire to write was too strong in him. Perkins couldn't, because the desire to be a famous writer was too strong."

"A year seems like a pretty short time to get all that depressed," said Levine.

Stonegell smiled. "When you're young," he said, "a year can be eternity. Patience is an attribute of the old."

"I suppose you're right. What about girl friends, other people who knew them both?"

"Well, there was one girl whom both were dating rather steadily. The rivalry again. I don't think either of them was particularly serious about her, but both of them wanted to take her away from the other one."

"Do you know this girl's name?"

"Yes, of course. She was in the same class with Perkins and Gruber. I think I might have her home address here."

Stonegell opened a small file drawer atop his desk, and looked through it. "Yes, here it is," he said. "Her name is Anne Marie Stone, and she lives on Grove Street, down in the Village. Here you are."

Levine accepted the card from Stonegell, copied the name and address onto his pad, and gave the card back. He got to his feet. "Thank you for your trouble," he said.

"Not at all," said Stonegell, standing. He extended his hand, and Levine, shaking it, found it bony and almost parchment-thin, but surprisingly strong. "I don't know if I've been much help, though," he said.

"Neither do I, yet," said Levine. "I may be just wasting both our time. Perkins confessed, after all."

"Still —" said Stonegell.

Levine nodded. "I know. That's what's got me doing extra work."

"I'm still thinking of this thing as though — as though it were a story problem, if you know what I mean. It isn't real yet. Two young students, I've taken an interest in both of them, fifty years after the worms get me they'll still be around—and then you tell me one of them is already wormfood, and the other one is effectively just as dead. It isn't real to me yet. They won't be in class tomorrow night, but I still won't believe it."

"I know what you mean."

"Let me know if anything happens, will you?"

"Of course."

Anne Marie Stone lived in an apartment on the fifth floor of a walk-up on Grove Street in Greenwich Village, a block and a half from Sheridan Square. Levine found himself out of breath by the time he reached the third floor, and he stopped for a minute to get his wind back and to slow the pounding of his heart. There was no sound in the world quite as loud as the beating of his own heart these days, and when that beating grew too rapid or too irregular, Detective Levine felt a kind of panic that twenty-four years as a cop had never been able to produce.

He had to stop again at the fourth floor, and he remembered with envy what a Bostonian friend had told him about a City of Boston regulation that buildings used as residence had to have elevators if they were more than four stories high. Oh, to live in Boston. Or, even better, in Levittown, where there isn't a building higher than two stories anywhere.

He reached the fifth floor, finally, and knocked on the door of apartment 5B. Rustlings from within culminated in the peephole in the door being opened, and a blue eye peered suspiciously out at him. "Who is it?" asked a muffled voice.

"Police," said Levine. He dragged out his wallet, and held it high, so the eye in the peephole could read the identification.

"Second," said the muffled voice, and the peephole closed. A seemingly endless series of rattles and clicks indicated locks being released, and then the door opened, and a short, slender girl, dressed in pink toreador pants, gray bulky sweater and blonde pony tail, motioned to Levine to come in. "Have a seat," she said, closing the door after him.

"Thank you." Levine sat in a new-fangled basket chair, as uncomfortable as it looked, and the girl sat in another chair of the same type, facing him. But she managed to look comfortable in the thing.

"Is this something I did?" she asked him. "Jaywalking or something?"

Levine smiled. No matter how innocent, a citizen always presumes himself guilty when the police come calling. "No," he said. "It concerns two friends of yours, Al Gruber and Larry Perkins."

"Those two?" The girl seemed calm, though curious, but not at all worried or apprehensive. She was still thinking in terms of something no more serious than jaywalking or a neighbor calling the police to complain about loud noises. "What are they up to?"

"How close are you to them?"

The girl shrugged. "I've gone out with both of them, that's all. We all take courses at Columbia. They're both nice guys, but there's nothing serious, you know. Not with either of them."

"I don't know how to say this," said Levine, "except the blunt way. Early this afternoon, Perkins turned himself in and admitted he'd just killed Gruber."

The girl stared at him. Twice, she opened her mouth to speak, but both times she closed it again. The silence lengthened, and Levine wondered belatedly if the girl had been telling the truth, if perhaps there had been something serious in her relationship with one of the boys after all. Then she blinked and looked away from him, clearing her throat. She stared out the window for a second, then looked back and said, "He's pulling your leg."

Levine shook his head. "I'm afraid not."

"Larry's got a wierd sense of humor sometimes," she said.

"It's a sick joke, that's all. Al's still around. You haven't found the body, have you?"

"I'm afraid we have. He was poisoned, and Perkins admitted he was the one who gave him the poison."

"That little bottle Al had around the place? That was only a gag."

"Not any more."

She thought about it a minute longer, then shrugged, as though giving up the struggle to either believe or disbelieve. "Why come to me?" she asked him.

"I'm not sure, to tell you the truth. Something smells wrong about the case, and I don't know what. There isn't any logic to it. I can't get through to Perkins, and it's too late to get through to Gruber. But I've got to get to know them both, if I'm going to understand what happened."

"And you want me to tell you about them."

"Yes."

"Where did you hear about me? From Larry?"

"No, he didn't mention you at all. The gentlemanly instinct, I suppose. I talked to your teacher, Professor Stonegell."

"I see." She stood up suddenly, in a single rapid and graceless movement, as though she had to make some motion, no matter how meaningless. "Do you want some coffee?"

"Thank you, yes."

"Come on along. We can talk while I get it ready."

He followed her through the apartment. A hallway led from the long, narrow living room past bedroom and bathroom to a tiny kitchen. Levine sat down at the kitchen table, and Anne Marie Stone went through the motions of making coffee. As she worked, she talked.

"They're good friends," she said. "I mean, they *were* good friends. You know what I mean. Anyway, they're a lot different from each other. Oh, golly! I'm getting all loused up in tenses."

"Talk as though both were still alive," said Levine. "It should be easier that way."

"I don't really believe it anyway," she said. "Al—he's a lot quieter than Larry. Kind of intense, you know? He's got a kind of reversed Messiah complex. You know, he figures he's supposed to be something great, a great writer, but he's afraid he doesn't have the stuff for it. So he worries about himself, and keeps trying to analyze himself, and he hates everything he writes because he doesn't think it's good enough for what he's supposed to be doing. That bottle of poison, that was a gag, you know, just a gag, but it was the kind of joke that has some sort of truth behind it. With this thing driving him like this, I suppose even death begins to look like a good escape after a while."

She stopped her preparations with the coffee, and stood listening to what she had just said. "Now he did escape, didn't he? I wonder if he'd thank Larry for taking the decision out of his hands."

"Do you suppose he asked Larry to take the decision out of his hands?"

She shook her head. "No. In the first place, Al could never ask anyone else to help him fight the thing out in any way. I know, I tried to talk to him a couple of times, but he just couldn't listen. It wasn't that he didn't want to listen, he just couldn't. He had to figure it out for himself. And Larry isn't the helpful sort, so Larry would be the last person anybody would go to for help. Not that Larry's a bad guy, really. He's just awfully self-centered. They both are, but in different ways. Al's always worried about himself, but Larry's always proud of himself. You know. Larry would say, 'I'm for me first,' and Al would say, 'Am I worthy?' Something like that."

"Had the two of them had a quarrel or anything recently, anything that you know of that might have prompted Larry to murder?"

"Not that I know of. They've both been getting more and

more depressed, but neither of them blamed the other. Al blamed himself for not getting anywhere, and Larry blamed the stupidity of the world. You know, Larry wanted the same thing Al did, but Larry didn't worry about whether he was worthy or capable or anything like that. He once told me he wanted to be a famous writer, and he'd be one if he had to rob banks and use the money to bribe every publisher and editor and critic in the business. That was a gag, too, like Al's bottle of poison, but I think that one had some truth behind it, too."

The coffee was ready, and she poured two cups, then sat down across from him. Levine added a bit of evaporated milk, but no sugar, and stirred the coffee distractedly. "I want to know why," he said. "Does that seem strange? Cops are supposed to want to know who, not why. I know who, but I want to know why."

"Larry's the only one who could tell you, and I don't think he will."

Levine drank some of the coffee, then got to his feet. "Mind if I use your phone?" he asked.

"Go right ahead. It's in the living room, next to the bookcase."

Levine walked back into the living room and called the station. He asked for Crawley. When his partner came on the line, Levine said, "Has Perkins signed the confession yet?"

"He's on the way down now. It's just been typed up."

"Hold him there after he signs it, okay? I want to talk to him. I'm in Manhattan, starting back now."

"What have you got?"

"I'm not sure I have anything. I just want to talk to Perkins again, that's all."

"Why sweat it? We got the body; we got the confession; we got the killer in a cell. Why make work for yourself?"

"I don't know. Maybe I'm just bored."

"Okay, I'll hold him. Same room as before."

Levine went back to the kitchen. "Thank you for the coffee," he said. "If there's nothing else you can think of, I'll be leaving now."

"Nothing," she said. "Larry's the only one can tell you why."

She walked him to the front door, and he thanked her again as he was leaving. The stairs were a lot easier going down.

When Levine got back to the station, he picked up another plainclothesman, a detective named Ricco, a tall, athletic man in his middle thirties who affected the Ivy League look. He resembled more closely someone from the District Attorney's office than a precinct cop. Levine gave him a part to play, and the two of them went down the hall to the room where Perkins was waiting with Crawley.

"Perkins," said Levine, the minute he walked in the room, before Crawley had a chance to give the game away by saying something to Ricco, "this is Dan Ricco, a reporter from the *Daily News*."

Perkins looked at Ricco with obvious interest, the first real display of interest and animation Levine had yet seen from him. "A reporter?"

"That's right," said Ricco. He looked at Levine. "What is this?" he asked. He was playing it straight and blank.

"College student," said Levine. "Name's Larry Perkins." He spelled the last name. "He poisoned a fellow student."

"Oh, yeah?" Ricco glanced at Perkins without much eagerness. "What for?" he asked, looking back at Levine. "Girl? Any sex in it?"

"Afraid not. It was some kind of intellectual motivation. They both wanted to be writers."

Ricco shrugged. "Two guys with the same job? What's so hot about that?"

"Well, the main thing," said Levine, "is that Perkins here wants to be famous. He tried to get famous by being a writer, but that wasn't working out. So he decided to be a famous murderer."

Ricco looked at Perkins. "Is that right?" he asked.

Perkins was glowering at them all, but especially at Levine. "What difference does it make?" he said.

"The kid's going to get the chair, of course," said Levine blandly. "We have his signed confession and everything. But I've kind of taken a liking to him. I'd hate to see him throw his life away without getting something for it. I thought maybe you could get him a nice headline on page two, something he could hang up on the wall of his cell."

Ricco chuckled and shook his head. "Not a chance of it," he said. "Even if I wrote the story big, the city desk would knock it down to nothing. This kind of story is a dime a dozen. People kill other people around New York twenty-four hours a day. Unless there's a good strong sex interest, or it's maybe one of those mass killings things like the guy who put the bomb in the airplane, a murder in New York is filler stuff. And who needs filler stuff in the spring, when the ball teams are just getting started?"

"You've got influence on the paper, Dan," said Levine. "Couldn't you at least get him picked up by the wire services?"

"Not a chance in a million. What's he done that a few hundred other clucks in New York don't do every year? Sorry, Abe, I'd like to do you the favor, but it's no go."

Levine sighed. "Okay, Dan," he said. "If you say so."

"Sorry," said Ricco. He grinned at Perkins. "Sorry, kid," he said. "You should of knifed a chorus girl or something."

Ricco left and Levine glanced at Crawley, who was industriously yanking on his ear-lobe and looking bewildered. Levine sat down facing Perkins and said, "Well?"

"Let me alone a minute," snarled Perkins. "I'm trying to think."

"I was right, wasn't I?" asked Levine. "You wanted to go out in a blaze of glory."

"All right, all right. Al took his way, I took mine. What's the difference?"

"No difference," said Levine. He got wearily to his feet, and headed for the door. "I'll have you sent back to your cell now."

"Listen," said Perkins suddenly. "You know I didn't kill him, don't you? You know he committed suicide, don't you?"

Levine opened the door and motioned to the two uniformed cops waiting in the hall.

"Wait," said Perkins desperately.

"I know, I know," said Levine. "Gruber really killed himself, and I suppose you burned the note he left."

"You know damn well I did."

"That's too bad, boy."

Perkins didn't want to leave. Levine watched deadpan as the boy was led away, and then he allowed himself to relax, let the tension drain out of him. He sagged into a chair and studied the veins on the backs of his hands.

Crawley said, into the silence, "What was all that about, Abe?"

"Just what you heard."

"Gruber committed suicide?"

"They both did."

"Well — what are we going to do now?"

"Nothing. We investigated; we got a confession; we made an arrest. Now we're done."

"But — "

"But hell!" Levine glared at his partner. "That little fool is gonna go to trial, Jack, and he's gonna be convicted and go to the chair. He chose it himself. It was *his* choice. I'm not railroading him; he chose his own end. And he's going to get what he wanted."

"But listen, Abe — "

"I won't listen!"

"Let me — let me get a word in."

Levine was on his feet suddenly, and now it all came

boiling out, the indignation and the rage and the frustration. "Damn it, you don't know yet! You've got another six, seven years yet. You don't know what it feels like to lie awake in bed at night and listen to your heart skip a beat every once in a while, and wonder when it's going to skip two beats in a row and you're dead. You don't know what it feels like to know your body's starting to die, it's starting to get old and die and it's all downhill from now on."

"What's that got to do with —"

"I'll tell you what! They had the *choice!* Both of them young, both of them with sound bodies and sound hearts and years ahead of them, decades ahead of them. And they chose to throw it away! They chose to throw away what I don't have any more. Don't you think I wish *I* had that choice? All right! They chose to die, let 'em die!"

Levine was panting from exertion, leaning over the desk and shouting in Jack Crawley's face. And now, in the sudden silence while he wasn't speaking, he heard the ragged rustle of his breath, felt the tremblings of nerve and muscle throughout his body. He let himself carefully down into a chair and sat there, staring at the wall, trying to get his breath.

Jack Crawley was saying something, far away, but Levine couldn't hear him. He was listening to something else, the loudest sound in all the world. The fitful throbbing of his own heart.

COME BACK, COME BACK

Detective Abraham Levine of Brooklyn's Forty-Third Precinct was a worried and a frightened man. He sat moodily at his desk in the small office he shared with his partner, Jack Crawley, and pensively drew lopsided circles on the back of a blank accident report form. In the approximate center of each circle he placed a dot, drew two lines out from the dot to make a clockface, reading three o'clock. An eight and a half by eleven sheet of white paper, covered with clock-faces, all reading three o'clock.

"That the time you see the doctor?"

Levine looked up, startled, called back from years away. Crawley was standing beside the desk, looking down at him, and Levine blinked, not having heard the question.

Crawley reached down and tapped the paper with a horny fingernail. "Three o'clock," he explained. "That the time you see the doctor?"

"Oh," said Levine. "Yes. Three o'clock."

33

Crawley said, "Take it easy, Abe."

"Sure," said Levine. He managed a weak smile. "No sense worrying beforehand, huh?"

"My brother," said Crawley, "he had one of those cardiograph things just a couple of months ago. He's just around your age, and man, he was worried. And the doctor tells him, 'You'll live to be a hundred.'"

"And then you'll die," said Levine.

"What the hell, Abe, we all got to go *sometime.*"

"Sure."

"Listen, Abe, you want to go on home? It's a dull day, nothing doing, I can — "

"Don't say that," Levine warned him. "The phone will ring." The phone rang as he was talking and he grinned, shrugging with palms up. "See?"

"Let me see what it is," said Crawley, reaching for the phone. "Probably nothing important. You can go on home and take it easy till three o'clock. It's only ten now and — Hello?" The last word spoken into the phone mouthpiece. "Yeah, this is Crawley."

Levine watched Crawley's face, trying to read in it the nature of the call. Crawley had been his partner for seven years, since old Jake Moshby had retired, and in that time they had become good friends, as close as two such different men could get to one another.

Crawley was a big man, somewhat overweight, somewhere in his middle forties. His clothes hung awkwardly on him, not as though they were too large or too small but as though they had been planned for a man of completely different proportions. His face was rugged, squarish, heavy-jowled. He looked like a tough cop, and he played the role very well.

Crawley had once described the quality of their partnership with reasonable accuracy. "With your brains and my beauty, Abe, we've got it made."

Now Levine watched Crawley's face as the big man

34

listened impassively to the phone, finally nodding and saying, "Okay, I'll go right on up there. Yeah, I know, that's what I figure, too." And he hung up.

"What is it, Jack?" Levine asked, getting up from the desk.

"A phony," said Crawley. "I can handle it, Abe. You go on home."

"I'd rather have some work to do. What is it?"

Crawley was striding for the door, Levine after him. "Man on a ledge," he said. "A phony. They're all phonies. The ones that really mean to jump do it right away, get it over with. Guys like this one, all they want is a little attention, somebody to tell them it's all okay, come on back in, everything's forgiven."

The two of them walked down the long green hall toward the front of the precinct. *Man on a ledge,* Levine thought. *Don't jump. Don't die. For God's sake, don't die.*

The address was an office building on Flatbush Avenue, a few blocks down from the bridge, near A&S and the major Brooklyn movie houses. A small crowd had gathered on the sidewalk across the street, looking up, but most of the pedestrians stopped only for a second or two, only long enough to see what the small crowd was gaping at, and then hurried on wherever they were going. They were still involved in life, they had things to do, they didn't have time to watch a man die.

Traffic on this side was being rerouted away from this block of Flatbush, around via Fulton or Willoughby or DeKalb. It was a little after ten o'clock on a sunny day in late June, warm without the humidity that would hit the city a week or two farther into the summer, but the uniformed cop who waved at them to make the turn was sweating, his blue shirt stained a darker blue, his forehead creased with strain above the sunglasses.

Crawley was driving their car, an unmarked black '56 Chevy, no siren, and he braked to a stop in front of the patrolman. He stuck his head and arm out the window, dangling his wallet open so the badge showed. "Precinct," he called.

"Oh," said the cop. He stepped aside to let them pass. "You didn't have any siren or light or anything," he explained.

"We don't want to make our friend nervous," Crawley told him.

The cop glanced up, then looked back at Crawley. "He's making *me* nervous," he said.

Crawley laughed. "A phony," he told the cop. "Wait and see."

On his side of the car, Levine had leaned his head out the window, was looking up, studying the man on the ledge.

It was an office building, eight stories high. Not a very tall building, particularly for New York, but plenty tall enough for the purposes of the man standing on the ledge that girdled the building at the sixth floor level. The first floor of the building was mainly a bank and partially a luncheonette. The second floor, according to the lettering strung along the front windows, was entirely given over to a loan company, and Levine could understand the advantage of the location. A man had his loan request turned down by the bank, all he had to do was go up one flight of stairs—or one flight in the elevator, more likely—and there was the loan company.

And if the loan company failed him too, there was a nice ledge on the sixth floor.

Levine wondered if this particular case had anything to do with money. Almost everything had something to do with money. Things that he became aware of because he was a cop, almost all of them had something to do with money. The psychoanalysts are wrong, he thought. It isn't sex that's at the center of all the pain in the world, it's money. Even when a cop answers a call from neighbors complaining about a couple screaming and fighting and throwing things at one another, nine times out of ten it's the same old thing they're arguing about. Money.

Levine's eyes traveled up the façade of the building, beyond the loan company's windows. None of the windows higher up bore the lettering of firm names. On the sixth floor, most of the windows were open, heads were sticking out into the air. And in the middle of it all, just out of reach of the windows on either side of him, was the man on the ledge.

Levine squinted, trying to see the man better against the brightness of the day. He wore a suit—it looked gray, but might be black—and a white shirt and dark tie, and the open suit coat and the tie were both whipping in the breeze up there. The man was standing as though crucified, back flat against the wall of the building, legs spread maybe two feet apart, arms out straight to either side of him, hands pressed palm-in against the stone surface of the wall.

The man was terrified. Levine was much too far away to see his face or read the expression there, but he didn't need any more than the posture of the body on the ledge. Taut, pasted to the wall, wide-spread. The man was terrified.

Crawley was right, of course. Ninety-nine times out of a hundred, the man on the ledge *is* a phony. He doesn't really expect to have to kill himself, though he will do it if pressed too hard. But he's out there on the ledge for one purpose and one purpose only: to be seen. He wants to be seen, he wants to be noticed. Whatever his unfulfilled demands on life, whatever his frustrations or problems, he wants other people to be forced to be aware of them, and to agree to help him overcome them.

If he gets satisfaction, he will allow himself, after a decent interval, to be brought back in. If he gets the raise, or the girl, or forgiveness from the boss for his embezzling, or forgiveness from his wife for his philandering, or whatever his one urgent demand is, once the demand is met, he will come in from the ledge.

But there is one danger he doesn't stop to think about, not until it's too late and he's already out there on the ledge, and the drama has already begun. The police know of this danger, and they know it is by far the greatest danger of the man on the ledge, much greater than any danger of deliberate self-destruction.

He can fall.

This one had learned that danger by now, as every inch of his straining taut body testified. He had learned it, and he was frightened out of his wits.

Levine grimaced. The man on the ledge didn't know — or if he knew, the knowledge was useless to him — that a terrified man can have an accident much more readily and much more quickly than a calm man. And so the man on the ledge always compounded his danger.

Crawley braked the Chevy to a stop at the curb, two doors beyond the address. The rest of the curb space was already used by official vehicles. An ambulance, white and gleaming. A smallish fire engine, red and full-packed with hose and ladders. A prowl car, most likely the one on this beat. The Crash & Rescue truck, dark blue, a first-aid station on wheels.

As he was getting out of the car, Levine noticed the firemen, standing around, leaning against the plate-glass windows of the bank, an eight foot net lying closed on the sidewalk near them. Levine took the scene in, and knew what had happened. The firemen had started to open the net. The man on the ledge had threatened to jump at once if they didn't take the net away. He could always jump to one side, miss the net. A net was no good unless the person to be caught *wanted* to be caught. So the firemen had closed up their net again, and now they were waiting, leaning against the bank windows, far enough away to the right.

Other men stood here and there on the sidewalk, some uniformed and some in plainclothes, most of them looking up at the man on the ledge. None of them stood inside a large white circle drawn in chalk on the pavement. It was a wide sidewalk here, in front of the bank, and the circle was almost the full width of it.

No one stood inside that circle because it marked the probable area where the man would land, if and when he fell or jumped from the ledge. And no one wanted to be underneath.

Crawley came around the Chevy, patting the fenders with a large calloused hand. He stopped next to Levine and looked up. "The phony," he growled, and Levine heard outrage in the tone. Crawley was an honest man, in simple terms of black and white. He hated dishonesty, in all its forms, from grand larceny to raucous television commercials. And a faked suicide attempt was dishonesty.

The two of them walked toward the building entrance. Crawley walked disdainfully through the precise center of the large chalked circle, not even bothering to look up. Levine walked around the outer edge.

Then the two of them went inside and took the elevator to the sixth floor.

The letters on the frosted-glass door read: "Anderson & Cartwright, Industrial Research Associates, Inc."

Crawley tapped on the glass. "Which one do you bet?" he asked. "Anderson or Cartwright?"

"It might be an employee."

Crawley shook his head. "Odds are against it. I take Anderson."

"Go in," said Levine gently. "Go on in."

Crawley pushed the door open and strode in, Levine behind him. It was the receptionist's office, cream-green walls and carpet, modernistic metal desk, modernistic metal and leather sofa and armchairs, modernistic saucer-shaped light fixtures hanging from bronzed chains attached to the ceiling.

Three women sat nervously, wide-eyed, off to the right, on the metal and leather armchairs. Above their heads were framed photographs of factory buildings, most of them in color, a few in black and white.

A uniformed patrolman was leaning against the receptionist's desk, arms folded across his chest, a relaxed expression on his face. He straightened up immediately when he saw Crawley and Levine. Levine recognized him as McCann, a patrolman working out of the same precinct.

"Am I glad to see you guys," said McCann. "Gundy's in talking to the guy now."

"Which one is it," Crawley asked, "Anderson or Cartwright?"

"Cartwright. Jason Cartwright. He's one of the bosses here."

Crawley turned a sour grin on Levine. "You win," he said, and led the way across the receptionist's office to the door marked: "JASON CARTWRIGHT PRIVATE."

There were two men in the room. One was sitting on the window ledge, looking out and to his left, talking in a soft voice. The other, standing a pace or two away from the windows, was the patrolman, Gundy. He and McCann would be the two from the prowl car, the first ones on the scene.

At their entrance, Gundy looked around and then came over to talk with them. He and McCann were cut from the same mold. Both young, tall, slender, thin-cheeked, ready to grin at a second's notice. The older a man gets, Levine thought, the longer it takes him to get a grin organized.

Gundy wasn't grinning now. He looked very solemn, and a little scared. Levine realized with shock that this might be Gundy's first brush with death. He didn't look as though he would have been out of the Academy very long.

I have news for you, Gundy, he thought. *You don't get used to it.*

Crawley said, "What's the story?"

"I'm not sure," said Gundy. "He went out there about twenty minutes ago. That's his son talking to him. Son's a lawyer, got an office right in this building."

"What's the guy out there want?"

Gundy shook his head. "He won't say. He just stands out

there. He won't say a word, except to shout that he's going to jump whenever anybody tries to get too close to him."

"A coy one," said Crawley, disgusted.

The phone shrilled, and Gundy stepped quickly over to the desk, picking up the receiver before the second ring. He spoke softly into the instrument, then looked over at the man by the window. "Your mother again," he said.

The man at the window spoke a few more words to the man on the ledge, then came over and took the phone from Gundy. Gundy immediately took his place at the window, and Levine could hear his first words plainly. "Just take it easy, now. Relax. But maybe you shouldn't close your eyes."

Levine looked at the son, now talking on the phone. A young man, not more than twenty-five or six. Blond crewcut, hornrim glasses, good mouth, strong jawline. Dressed in Madison Avenue conservative. Just barely out of law school, from the look of him.

Levine studied the office. It was a large room, eighteen to twenty feet square, as traditional as the outer office was contemporary. The desk was a massive piece of furniture, a dark warm wood, the legs and drawer faces carefully and intricately carved. Glass-faced bookshelves lined one complete wall. The carpet was a neutral gray, wall-to-wall. There were two sofas, brown leather, long and deep and comfortable-looking. Bronze ashtray stands. More framed photographs of plant buildings.

The son was saying, "Yes, mother. I've been talking to him, mother. I don't know, mother."

Levine walked over, said to the son, "May I speak to her for a minute, please?"

"Of course. Mother, there's a policeman here who wants to talk to you."

Levine accepted the phone, said, "Mrs. Cartwright?"

The voice that answered was high-pitched, and Levine could readily imagine it becoming shrill. The voice said, "Why is he out there? Why is he doing that?"

"We don't know yet," Levine told her. "We were hoping you might be able to —— "

"Me?" The voice was suddenly a bit closer to being shrill. "I still can't really believe this. I don't know why he'd — I have no idea. What does he say?"

"He hasn't told us why yet," said Levine. "Where are you now, Mrs. Cartwright?"

"At home, of course."

"That's where?"

"New Brunswick."

"Do you have a car there? Could you drive here now?"

"There? To New York?"

"It might help, Mrs. Cartwright, if he could see you, if you could talk to him."

"But — it would take *hours* to get there! Surely, it would be — that is, before I got there, you'd have him safe already, wouldn't you?"

She hopes he jumps, thought Levine, with sudden certainty. *By God, she hopes he jumps!*

"Well, wouldn't you?"

"Yes," he said wearily. "I suppose you're right. Here's your son again."

He extended the receiver to the son, who took it, cupped the mouthpiece with one hand, said worriedly, "Don't misunderstand her. Please, she isn't as cold as she might sound. She loves my father, she really does."

"All right," said Levine. He turned away from the pleading in the son's eyes, said to Crawley, "Let's talk with him a bit."

"Right," said Crawley.

There were two windows in the office, about ten feet apart, and Jason Cartwright was standing directly between them on the ledge. Crawley went to the left-hand window and Levine to the right-hand window, where the patrolman Gundy was still trying to chat with the man on the ledge, trying to keep him distracted from the height and his desire to jump. "We'll take over," Levine said softly, and Gundy nodded gratefully and backed away from the window.

Levine twisted around, sat on the windowsill, hooked one arm under the open window, leaned out slightly so that the breeze touched his face. He looked down.

Six stories. God, who would have thought six stories was so high from the ground? This is the height when you really get the feeling of height. On top of the Empire State building, or flying in a plane, it's just too damn high, it isn't real any more. But six stories—that's a fine height to be at, to really understand the terror of falling.

Place ten Levines, one standing on another's shoulders, forming a human tower or a totem pole, and the Levine in the window wouldn't be able to reach the cropped gray hair on the head of the top Levine in the totem pole.

Down there, he could make out faces, distinguish eyes and open mouths, see the blue jeans and high boots and black slickers of the firemen, the red domes atop the police cars. Across the street, he could see the red of a girl's sweater.

He looked down at the street, sixty-six feet below him. It was a funny thing about heights, a strange and funny and terrifying thing. Stand by the rail of a bridge, looking down at the water. Stand by a window on the sixth floor, looking down at the street. And from miles down inside the brain, a filthy little voice snickers and leers and croons, "Jump. Go on and jump. Wouldn't you like to know how it would feel, to fall free through space? Go on, go on, jump."

From his left, Crawley's voice suddenly boomed out. "Aren't you a little old, Cartwright, for this kind of nonsense?"

The reassuring well-known reality of Crawley's voice tore Levine away from the snickering little voice. He suddenly realized he'd been leaning too far out from the window, and pulled himself hastily back.

And he felt his heart pounding within his chest. Three

o'clock, he had to go see that doctor. He had to be calm; his heart had to be calm for the doctor's inspection.

At night — He didn't get enough sleep at night any more, that was part of the problem. But it was impossible to sleep and listen to one's heart at the same time, and of the two it was more important to listen to the heart. Listen to it plodding along, laboring, like an old man climbing a hill with a heavy pack. And then, all at once, the silence. The skipped beat. And the sluggish heart gathering its forces, building its strength, plodding on again. It had never yet skipped two beats in a row.

It could only do that once.

"What is it you want, Cartwright?" called Crawley's voice.

Levine, for the first time, looked to the left and saw Jason Cartwright.

A big man, probably an athlete in his younger days, still muscular but now padded with the flesh of years. Black hair with a natural wave in it, now mussed by the breeze. A heavy face, the chin sagging a bit but the jawline still strong, the nose large and straight, the forehead wide, the brows out-thrust, the eyes deep and now wide and wild. A good-looking man, probably in his late forties.

Levine knew a lot about him already. From the look of the son in there, this man had married young, probably while still in his teens. From the sound of the wife, the marriage had soured. From the look of the office and the apparent education of the son, his career had blossomed where his marriage hadn't. So this time, one of the exceptions, the trouble wouldn't be money. This time, it was connected most likely with his marriage.

Another woman?

It wouldn't be a good idea to ask him. Sooner or later, he would state his terms, he would tell them what had driven him out here. Force the issue, and he might jump. A man on a ledge goes out there not wanting to jump, but accepting the fact that he may have to.

Cartwright had been looking at Crawley, and now he turned his head, stared at Levine. "Oh, no you don't!" he cried. His voice would normally be baritone, probably a pleasant speaking voice, but emotion had driven it up the scale, making it raucuous, tinged with hysteria. "One distracts me while the other sneaks up on me, is that it?" the man cried. "You won't get away with it. Come near me and I'll jump, I swear I'll jump!"

"I'll stay right here," Levine promised. Leaning far out, he would be almost able to reach Cartwright's out-stretched hand. But if he were to touch it, Cartwright would surely jump. And if he were to grip it, Cartwright would most likely drag him along too, all the way down to the sidewalk sixty-six feet below.

"What is it, Cartwright?" demanded Crawley again. "What do you want?"

Way back at the beginning of their partnership, Levine and Crawley had discovered the arrangement that worked best for them. Crawley asked the questions, and Levine listened to the answers. While a man paid attention to Crawley, erected his façade between himself and Crawley, Levine, silent and unnoticed, could come in on the flank, peek behind the façade and see the man who was really there.

"I want you to leave me alone!" cried Cartwright. "Everybody, everybody! Just leave me alone!"

"Look up at the sky, Mister Cartwright," said Levine softly, just loud enough for the man on the ledge to hear him. "Look how blue it is. Look down across the street. Do you see the red of that girl's sweater? Breathe in, Mister Cartwright. Do you smell the city? Hark! Listen! Did you hear that car-horn? That was over on Fulton Street, wasn't it?"

"Shut up!" screamed Cartwright, turning swiftly, precariously, to glare again at Levine. "Shut up, shut up, shut up. Leave me alone!"

Levine knew all he needed. "Do you want to talk to your son?" he asked.

"Allan?" The man's face softened all at once. "Allan?"

"He's right here," said Levine. He came back in from the window, signalled to the son, who was no longer talking on the phone. "He wants to talk to you."

The son rushed to the window. "Dad?"

Crawley came over, glowering. "Well?" he said.

Levine shook his head. "He doesn't want to die."

"I know that. What now?"

"I think it's the wife." Levine motioned to Gundy, who came over, and he said, "Is the partner here? Anderson?"

"Sure," said Gundy. "He's in his office. He tried to talk to Cartwright once, but Cartwright got too excited. We thought it would be a good idea if Anderson kept out of sight."

"Who thought? Anderson?"

"Well, yes. All of us. Anderson and McCann and me."

"Okay," said Levine. "You and the boy—what's his name, Allan?—stay here. Let me know what's happening, if anything at all does happen. We'll go talk with Mister Anderson now."

Anderson was short, slender, very brisk, very bald. His wire-framed spectacles reflected light, and his round little face was troubled. "No warning at all," he said. "Not a word. All of a sudden, Joan—she's our receptionist—got a call from someone across the street, saying there was a man on the ledge. And it was Jason. Just like that! No warning at all."

"The sign on your door," said Crawley, "says Industrial Research. What's that, efficiency expert stuff?"

Anderson smiled, a quick nervous flutter. "Not exactly," he said. He was devoting all his attention to Crawley, who was standing directly in front of him and who was asking the questions. Levine stood to one side, watching the movements of Anderson's lips and eyes and hands as he spoke.

"We are efficiency experts, in a way," Anderson was saying, "but not in the usual sense of the term. We don't work with time-charts, or how many people should work in the steno pool, things like that. Our major concern is the physical plant itself, the structure and design of the plant buildings and work areas."

Crawley nodded. "Architects," he said.

Anderson's brief smile fluttered on his face again, and he shook his head. "No, we work in conjunction with the architect, if it's a new building. But most of our work is concerned with the modernization of old facilities. In a way, we're a central clearing agency for new ideas in industrial plant procedures." It was, thought Levine, an explanation Anderson was used to making, so used to making that it sounded almost like a memorized patter.

"You and Cartwright equal partners?" asked Crawley. It was clear he hadn't understood a word of Anderson's explanation and was impatient to move on to other things.

Anderson nodded. "Yes, we are. We've been partners for twenty-one years."

"You should know him well, then."

"I should think so, yes."

"Then maybe you know why he suddenly decided to go crawl out on the ledge."

Eyes widening, Anderson shook his head again. "Not a thing," he said. "I had no idea, nothing, I — There just wasn't any warning at all."

Levine stood off to one side, watching, his lips pursed in concentration. Was Anderson telling the truth? It seemed likely; it *felt* likely. The marriage again. It kept going back to the marriage.

"Has he acted at all funny lately?" Crawley was still pursuing the same thought, that there had to be some previous build-up, and that the build-up should show. "Has he been moody, anything like that?"

"Jason—" Anderson stopped, shook his head briefly, started again. "Jason is a quiet man, by nature. He—he rarely uh, *forces* his personality, if you know what I mean. If he's been thinking about this, whatever it is, it—it wouldn't show. I don't *think* it would show."

"Would he have any business worries at all?" Crawley undoubtedly realized by now this was a blind alley, but he would go through the normal questions anyway. You never could tell.

Anderson, as was to be expected, said, "No, none. We've—well, we've been doing very well. The last five years, we've been expanding steadily, we've even added to our staff, just six months ago."

Levine now spoke for the first time. "What about Mrs. Cartwright?" he asked.

Anderson looked blank, as he turned to face Levine. "Mrs. Cartwright? I—I don't understand what you mean."

Crawley immediately picked up the new ball, took over the questioning again. "Do you know her well, Mister Anderson? What kind of woman would you say she was?"

Anderson turned back to Crawley, once again opening his flank to Levine. "She's, well, actually I haven't seen very much of her the last few years. Jason moved out of Manhattan five, six years ago, over to Jersey, and I live out on the Island, so we don't, uh, we don't *socialize* very much, as much as we used to. As you get older—" he turned to face Levine, as though instinctively understanding that Levine would more readily know what he meant "—you don't go out so much any more, in the evening. You don't, uh, keep up friendships as much as you used to."

"You must know *something* about Mrs. Cartwright," said Crawley.

Anderson gave his attention to Crawley again. "She's, well, I suppose the best way to describe her is *determined*. I know for a fact she was the one who talked Jason into coming into partnership with me, twenty-one years ago. A forceful woman. Not a nag, mind you, I don't mean that at all. A very pleasant woman really. A good hostess. A good mother, from the look of Allan. But forceful."

The wife, thought Levine. *She's the root of it. She knows, too, what drove him out there.*

And she wants him to jump.

Back in Cartwright's office, the son Allan was once again at the phone. The patrolman Gundy was at the left-hand window, and a new man, in clerical garb, at the right-hand window.

Gundy noticed Levine and Crawley come in, and immediately left the window. "A priest," he said softly. "Anderson said he was Catholic, so we got in touch with St. Marks, over on Willoughby."

Levine nodded. He was listening to the son. "I don't know, mother. Of course, mother, we're doing everything we can. No, mother, no reporters up here, maybe it won't have to be in the papers at all."

Levine went over to the window Gundy had vacated, took up a position where he could see Cartwright, carefully refrained from looking down at the ground. The priest was saying, "God has his time for you, Mister Cartwright. This is God's prerogative, to choose the time and the means of your death."

Cartwright shook his head, not looking at the priest, glaring instead directly across Flatbush Avenue at the building across the way. "There is no God," he said.

"I don't believe you mean that, Mister Cartwright," said the priest. "I believe you've lost your faith in yourself, but I don't believe you've lost faith in God."

"Take that away!" screamed Cartwright all at once. "Take that away, or I jump right now!"

He was staring down toward the street, and Levine followed the direction of his gaze. Poles had been extended from windows on the floor below, and a safety net, similar to that used by circus performers, was being unrolled along them.

"Take that away!" screamed Cartwright again. He was leaning precariously forward, his face mottled red with fury and terror.

"Roll that back in!" shouted Levine. "Get it out of there, he can jump over it! Roll it back in!"

A face jutted out of one of the fifth-floor windows, turning inquiringly upward, saying, "Who are you?"

"Levine. Precinct. Get that thing away from there."

"Right you are," said the face, making it clear he accepted no responsibility either way. And the net and poles were withdrawn.

The priest, on the other side, was saying, "It's all right. Relax, Mr. Cartwright; it's all right. These people only want to help you; it's all right." The priest's voice was shaky. Like Gundy, he was a rookie at this. He'd never been asked to talk in a suicide before.

Levine twisted around, looking up. Two stories up, and the roof. More men were up there, with another safety net. If this were the top floor, they would probably take a chance with that net, try flipping it over him and pasting him like a butterfly to the wall. But not here, three stories down.

Cartwright had turned his face away from the still-talking priest, was studying Levine intently. Levine returned his gaze, and Cartwright said, "Where's Laura? She should be here by now, shouldn't she? Where is she?"

"Laura? You mean your wife?"

"Of course," he said. He stared at Levine, trying to read something to Levine's face. "Where is she?"

Tell him the truth? No. Tell him his wife wasn't coming, and he would jump right away. "She's on the way," he said. "She should be here pretty soon."

Cartwright turned his face forward again, stared off across the street. The priest was still talking, softly, insistently.

Levine came back into the office. To Crawley, he said, "It's the wife. He's waiting for her."

"They've always got a wife," said Crawley sourly. "And there's always just the one person they'll tell it to. Well, how long before she gets here?"

"She isn't coming."

"What?"

"She's at home, over in Jersey. She said she wouldn't come." Levine shrugged and added, "I'll try her again."

The son was still on the phone, but he handed it over as soon as Levine spoke to him. Levine said, "This is Detective Levine again, Mrs. Cartwright. We'd like you to come down here after all, please. Your husband asked to talk to you."

There was hesitation from the woman for a few seconds, and then she burst out, "Why can't you bring him in? Can't you even *stop* him?"

"He's out of reach, Mrs. Cartwright. If we tried to get him, I'm afraid he'd jump."

"This is ridiculous! No, no, definitely not, I'm not going to be a party to it. I'm not going to talk to him until he comes in from there. You tell him that."

"Mrs. Cartwright ——"

"I'm not going to have any more to do with it!"

The click was loud in Levine's ear as she slammed the receiver onto the hook. Crawley was looking at him, and now said, "Well?"

"She hung up."

"She isn't coming?" It was plain that Crawley was having trouble believing it.

Levine glanced at the son, who could hear every word he was saying, and then shrugged. "She wants him to jump," he said.

The son's reaction was much smaller than Levine had expected. He simply shook his head definitely and said, "No."

Levine waited, looking at him.

The son shook his head again. "That isn't true," he said. "She just doesn't understand—she doesn't really think he means it."

"All right," said Levine. He turned away from the son, trying to think. The wife, the marriage—A man in his late forties, married young, son grown and set up in his own vocation. A quiet man, who doesn't force his personality on others, and a forceful wife. A practical wife, who pushed him into a successful business.

Levine made his decision. He nodded, and went back through the receptionist's office, where the other patrolman, McCann, was chatting with the three women employees. Levine went into Anderson's office, said, "Excuse me. Could I have the use of your office for a little while?"

"Certainly." Anderson got up from his desk, came around, saying, "Anything at all, anything at all."

"Thank you."

Levine followed Anderson back to the receptionist's office, looked over the three women sitting against the left-hand wall. Two were fortyish, plumpish, wearing wedding bands. The third looked to be in her early thirties, was tall and slender, good-looking in a solid level-eyed way, not glamorous. She wore no rings at all.

Levine went over to the third woman, said, "Could I speak to you for a minute, please?"

She looked up, startled, a bit frightened. "What? Oh. Oh, yes, of course."

She followed him back into Anderson's office. He motioned her to the chair facing Anderson's desk, himself sat behind the desk. "My name is Levine," he said. "Detective Abraham Levine. And you are——?"

"Janice Shale," she said. Her voice was low, pleasantly melodious. She was wearing normal office clothing, a gray plain skirt and white plain blouse.

"You've worked here how long?"

"Three years." She was answering readily enough, with no hesitations, but deep in her eyes he could see she was frightened, and wary.

"Mister Cartwright won't tell us why he wants to kill himself," he began. "He's asked to speak to his wife, but she refuses to leave home —" He detected a tightening of her lips when he said that. Disapproval of Mrs. Cartwright? He went on. "— which we haven't told him yet. He doesn't really want to jump, Miss Shale. He's a frustrated, thwarted man. There's something he wants or needs that he can't get, and he's chosen this way to try to force the issue." He paused, studying her face, said, "Would that something be you?"

Color started in her cheeks, and she opened her mouth for what he knew would be an immediate denial. But the denial didn't come. Instead, Janice Shale sagged in the chair, defeated and miserable, not meeting Levine's eyes. In a small voice, barely audible, she said, "I didn't think he'd do anything like this. I never thought he'd do anything like this."

"He wants to marry you, is that it? And he can't get a divorce."

The girl nodded, and all at once she began to cry. She wept with one closed hand pressed to her mouth, muffling the sound, her head bowed as though she were ashamed of this weakness, ashamed to be seen crying.

Levine waited, watching her with the dulled helplessness of a man whose job by its very nature kept him exposed to the misery and frustrations of others. He would always want to help, and he would always be unable to help, to really help.

Janice Shale controlled herself, slowly and painfully. When she looked up again, Levine knew she was finished weeping, no matter what happened. "What do you want me to do?" she said.

"Talk to him. His wife won't come — she knows what he wants to say to her, I suppose — so you're the only one."

"What can I say to him?"

Levine felt weary, heavy. Breathing, working the heart, pushing the sluggish blood through veins and arteries, was wearing, hopeless, exhausting labor. "I don't know," he said. "He wants to die because of you. Tell him why he should live."

Levine stood by the right-hand window, just out of sight of the man on the ledge. The son and the priest and Crawley and Gundy were all across the room, watching and waiting, the son looking bewildered, the priest relieved, Crawley sour, Gundy excited.

Janice Shale was at the left-hand window, tense and frightened. She leaned out, looking down, and Levine saw her body go rigid, saw her hands tighten on the window-frame. She closed her eyes, swaying, inhaling, and Levine stood ready to move. If she were to faint from that position, she could fall out the window.

But she didn't faint. She raised her head and opened her eyes, and carefully avoided looking down at the street again. She looked, instead, to her right, toward the man on the ledge. "Jay," she said. "Jay, please."

"Jan!" Cartwright sounded surprised. "What are you doing? Jan, go back in there, stay away from this. Go back in there."

Levine stood by the window, listening. What would she say to him? What *could* she say to him?

"Jay," she said, slowly, hesitantly, "Jay, please. It isn't worth it. Nothing is worth — dying for."

"Where's Laura?"

Levine waited, unbreathing, and at last the girl spoke the lie he had placed in her mouth. "She's on the way. She'll be here soon. But what does it matter, Jay? She still won't agree, you know that. She won't believe you."

"I'll wait for Laura," he said.

The son was suddenly striding across the room, shouting, "What is this? What's going on here?"

Levine spun around, motioning angrily for the boy to be quiet.

"Who is that woman?" demanded the son. "What's she doing here?"

Levine intercepted him before he could get to Janice Shale, pressed both palms flat against the boy's shirt-front. "Get back over there," he whispered fiercely. "Get back over there."

"Get away from me! Who is she? What's going on here?"

"Allan?" It was Cartwright's voice, shouting the question. "Allan?"

Crawley now had the boy's arms from behind, and he and Levine propelled him toward the door. "Let me *go!*" cried the boy. "I've got a right to ——"

Crawley's large hand clamped across his mouth, and the three of them barreled through to the receptionist's office. As the door closed behind them, Levine heard Janice Shale repeating, "Jay? Listen to me, Jay, please. Please, Jay."

The door safely shut behind them, the two detectives let the boy go. He turned immediately, trying to push past them and get back inside, crying, "You can't do this! Let me go! What do you think you are? Who is that woman?"

"Shut up," said Levine. He spoke softly, but the boy quieted at once. In his voice had been all his own miseries, all his own frustrations, and his utter weariness with the misery and frustration of others.

"I'll tell you who that woman is," Levine said. "She's the woman your father wants to marry. He wants to divorce your mother and marry her."

"No," said the boy, as sure and positive as he had been earlier in denying that his mother would want to see his father dead.

"Don't say no," said Levine coldly. "I'm telling you facts.

That's what sent him out there on that ledge. Your mother won't agree to the divorce."

"My mother——"

"Your mother," Levine pushed coldly on, "planned your father's life. Now, all at once, he's reached the age where he should have accomplished whatever he set out to do. His son is grown, he's making good money, now's the time for him to look around and say, 'This is the world I made for myself, and it's a good one.' But he can't. Because he doesn't like his life, it isn't *his* life, it's the life your mother planned for him."

"You're wrong," said the boy. "You're wrong."

"So he went looking." said Levine, ignoring the boy's interruptions, "and he found Janice Shale. She wouldn't push him, she wouldn't plan for him, she'd let *him* be the strong one."

The boy just stood here, shaking his head, repeating over and over, "You're wrong. You're wrong."

Levine grimaced, in irritation and defeat. *You never break through,* he thought. *You never break through.* Aloud he said, "In twenty years you'll believe me." He looked over at the patrolman, McCann. "Keep this young man out here with you," he said.

"Right," said McCann.

"Why?" cried the son. "He's my father! Why can't I go in there?"

"Shame," Levine told him. "If he saw his son and this woman at the same time, he'd jump."

The boy's eyes widened. He started to shake his head, then just stood there, staring.

Levine and Crawley went back into the other room.

Janice Shale was coming away from the window, her face ashen. "Somebody down on the sidewalk started taking pictures," she said. "Jay shouted at them to stop. He told me to get in out of sight, or he'd jump right now."

"Respectability," said Levine, as through the word were obscene. "We're all fools."

Crawley said, "Think we ought to send someone for the wife?"

"No. She'd only make it worse. She'd say no, and he'd go over."

"Oh God!" Janice Shale swayed suddenly and Crawley grabbed her arm, led her across to one of the leather sofas.

Levine went back to the right-hand window. He looked out. A block away, on the other side of the street, there was a large clock in front of a bank building. It was almost eleven-thirty. They'd been here almost an hour and a half.

Three o'clock, he thought suddenly. This thing had to be over before three o'clock, that was the time of his appointment with the doctor.

He looked out at Cartwright. The man was getting tired. His face was drawn with strain and emotion, and his fingertips were clutching tight to the rough face of the wall. Levine said, "Cartwright."

The man turned his head, slowly, afraid now of rapid movement. He looked at Levine without speaking.

"Cartwright," said Levine. "Have you thought about it now? Have you thought about death?"

"I want to talk to my wife."

"You could fall before she got here," Levine told him. "She has a long way to drive, and you're getting tired. Come in, come in here. You can talk to her in here when she arrives. You've proved your point, man, you can come in. Do you want to get too tired, do you want to lose your balance, lose your footing, slip and fall?"

"I want to talk to my wife," he said, doggedly.

"Cartwright, you're *alive.*" Levine stared helplessly at the man, searching for the way to tell him how precious that was, the fact of being alive. "You're breathing," he said. "You can see and hear and smell and taste and touch. You can laugh at jokes, you can love a woman — For God's sake man, you're *alive!*"

Cartwright's eyes didn't waver; his expression didn't change. "I want to talk to my wife," he repeated.

"Listen," said Levine. "You've been out here two hours now. You've had time to think about death, about non-being. Cartwright, listen. Look at me, Cartwright, I'm going to the doctor at three o'clock this afternoon. He's going to tell me about my heart, Cartwright. He's going to tell me if my heart is getting too tired. He's going to tell me if I'm going to stop being alive."

Levine strained with the need to tell this fool what he was throwing away, and knew it was hopeless.

The priest was back, all at once, at the other window. "Can we help you?" he asked. "Is there anything any of us can do to help you?"

Cartwright's head swiveled slowly. He studied the priest. "I want to talk to my wife," he said.

Levine gripped the windowsill. There had to be a way to bring him in, there had to be a way to trick him or force him or convince him to come in. He had to be brought in, he couldn't throw his life away, that's the only thing a man really has.

Levine wished desperately that *he* had the choice.

He leaned out again suddenly, glaring at the back of Cartwright's head. "Jump!" he shouted.

Cartwright's head swiveled around, the face open, the eyes shocked, staring at Levine in disbelief.

"Jump!" roared Levine. "Jump, you damn fool, end it, stop being alive, *die! Jump!* Throw yourself away, you imbecile, JUMP!"

Wide-eyed, Cartwright stared at Levine's flushed face, looked out and down at the crowd, the fire truck, the ambulance, the uniformed men, the chalked circle on the pavement.

And all at once he began to cry. His hands came up to his

face, he swayed, and the crowd down below sighed, like a breeze rustling. "God help me!" Cartwright screamed.

Crawley came swarming out the other window, his legs held by Gundy. He grabbed for Cartwright's arm, growling, "All right, now, take it easy. Take it easy. This way, this way, just slide your feet along, don't try to bring the other foot around, just slide over, easy, easy——"

And the man came stumbling in from the ledge.

"You took a chance," said Crawley. "You took one hell of a chance." It was two-thirty, and Crawley was driving him to the doctor's office.

"I know," said Levine. His hands were still shaking; he could still feel the ragged pounding of his heart within his chest.

"But you called his bluff," said Crawley. "That kind, it's just a bluff. They don't really want to dive, they're bluffing."

"I know," said Levine.

"But you still took a hell of a chance."

"It——" Levine swallowed. It felt as though there were something hard caught in his throat. "It was the only way to get him in," he said. "The wife wasn't coming, and nothing else would bring him in. When the girlfriend failed——"

"It took guts, Abe. For a second there, I almost thought he was going to take you up on it."

"So did I."

Crawley pulled in at the curb in front of the doctor's office. "I'll pick you up around quarter to four," he said.

"I can take a cab," said Levine.

"Why? Why for the love of Mike? The city's paying for the gas."

Levine smiled at his partner. "All right," he said. He got out of the car, went up the walk, up the stoop, onto the front porch. He looked back, watched the Chevvy turn the corner. He whispered, "I *wanted* him to jump."

Then he went in to find out if he was going to stay alive.

THE FEEL
OF THE TRIGGER

Abraham Levine, Detective of Brooklyn's Forty-third Precinct, sat at a desk in the squadroom and worriedly listened to his heart skip every eighth beat. It was two o'clock on Sunday morning, and he had the sports section of the *Sunday Times* open on the desk, but he wasn't reading it. He hadn't been reading it for about ten minutes now. Instead, he'd been listening to his heart.

A few months ago, he'd discovered the way to listen to his heart without anybody knowing he was doing it. He'd put his right elbow on the desk and press the heel of his right hand to his ear, hard enough to cut out all outside sound. At first it would sound like underwater that way, and then gradually he would become aware of a regular clicking sound. It wasn't a beating or a thumping or anything like that, it was a click-click-click-click — click-click-

There it was again. Nine beats before the skip that time. It fluctuated between every eighth beat and every twelfth beat.

The doctor had told him not to worry about that, lots of people had it, but that didn't exactly reassure him. Lots of people died of heart attacks, too. Lots of people around the age of fifty-three.

"Abe? Don't you feel good?"

Levine guiltily lowered his hand. He looked over at his shift partner, Jack Crawley, sitting with the *Times* crossword puzzle at another desk. "No, I'm okay," he said. "I was just thinking."

"About your heart?"

Levine wanted to say no, but he couldn't. Jack knew him too well.

Crawley got to his feet, stretching, a big bulky harness bull. "You're a hypochondriac, Abe," he said. "You're a good guy, but you got an obsession."

"You're right." He grinned sheepishly. "I almost wish the phone would ring."

Crawley mangled a cigarette out of the pack. "You went to the doctor, didn't you? A couple of months ago. And what did he tell you?"

"He said I had nothing to worry about," Levine admitted. "My blood pressure is a little high, that's all." He didn't want to talk about the skipping.

"So there you are," said Crawley reasonably. "You're still on duty, aren't you? If you had a bum heart, they'd retire you, right?"

"Right."

"So relax. And don't hope for the phone to ring. This is a quiet Saturday night. I've been waiting for this one for years."

The Saturday night graveyard shift—Sunday morning, actually, midnight till eight—was usually the busiest shift in the week. Saturday night was the time when normal people got violent, and violent people got murderous, the time when precinct plainclothesmen were usually on the jump.

Tonight was unusual. Here it was, after two o'clock, and

only one call so far, a bar hold-up over on 23rd. Rizzo and McFarlane were still out on that one, leaving Crawley and Levine to mind the store and read the *Times*.

Crawley now went back to the crossword puzzle, and Levine made an honest effort to read the sports section.

They read in silence for ten minutes, and then the phone rang on Crawley's desk. Crawley scooped the receiver up to his ear, announced himself, and listened.

The conversation was brief. Crawley's end of it was limited to yesses and got-its, and Levine waited, watching his wrestler's face, trying to read there what the call was about.

Then Crawley broke the connection by depressing the cradle buttons, and said, over his shoulder, "Hold-up. Grocery store at Green and Tanahee. Owner shot. That was the beat cop, Wills."

Levine got heavily to his feet and crossed the squadroom to the coatrack, while Crawley dialed a number and said, "Emergency, please."

Levine shrugged into his coat, purposely not listening to Crawley's half of the conversation. It was brief enough, anyway. When Crawley came over to get his own coat, he said, "DOA. Four bullets in him. One of these trigger-happy amateurs."

"Any witnesses?"

"Wife. The beat man—Wills—says she thinks she recognized the guy."

"Widow," said Levine.

Crawley said, "What?"

Widow. Not wife any more, widow. "Nothing," said Levine.

If you're a man fifty-three years of age, there's a statistical chance your heart will stop this year. But there's no sense getting worried about it. There's an even better statistical chance that it *won't* stop this year. So, if you go to the doctor and he says don't worry, then you shouldn't worry. Don't think morbid thoughts. Don't think about death all the time, think about life. Think about your work, for instance.

But what if it so happens that your work, as often as not, is death? What if you're a precinct detective, the one the wife calls when her husband just keeled over at the breakfast table, the one the hotel calls for the guest who never woke up this morning? What if the short end of the statistics is that end you most often see?

Levine sat in the squad car next to Crawley, who was driving, and looked out at the Brooklyn streets, trying to distract his mind. At two A.M. Brooklyn is dull, with red neon signs and grimy windows in narrow streets. Levine wished he'd taken the wheel.

They reached the intersection of Tanahee and Green, and Crawley parked in a bus-stop zone. They got out of the car.

The store wasn't exactly on the corner. It was two doors down Green, on the southeast side, occupying the ground floor of a red-brick tenement building. The plate-glass window was filthy, filled with show-boxes of Kellogg's Pep and Tide and Premium Saltines. Inevitably, the letters SALADA were curved across the glass. The flap of the rolled-up green awning above the window had lettering on it, too: *Fine Tailoring.*

There were two slate steps up, and then the store. The glass in the door was so covered with cigarette and soft-drink decals it was almost impossible to see inside. On the reverse, they all said, "Thank you — call again."

The door was closed now, and locked. Levine caught a glimpse of blue uniform through the decals, and rapped softly on the door. The young patrolman, Wills, recognized him and pulled the door open. "Stanton's with her," he said. "In back." He meant the patrolman from the prowl car parked now out front.

Crawley said, "You got any details yet?"

"On what happened," said Wills, "yes."

Levine closed and locked the door again, and turned to listen.

"There weren't any customers," Wills was saying. "The store stays open till three in the morning, weekends. Midnight during the week. It was just the old couple—Kosofsky, Nathan and Emma—they take turns, and they both work when it's busy. The husband—Nathan—he was out here, and his wife was in back, making a pot of tea. She heard the bell over the door——"

"Bell?" Levine turned and looked up at the top of the door. There hadn't been any bell sound when they'd come in just now.

"The guy ripped it off the wall on his way out."

Levine nodded. He could see the exposed wood where screws had been dragged out. Somebody tall, then, over six foot. Somebody strong, and nervous, too.

"She heard the bell," said Wills, "and then, a couple minutes later, she heard the shots. So she came running out, and saw this guy at the cash register——"

"She saw him," said Crawley.

"Yeah, sure. But I'll get to that in a minute. Anyway, he took a shot at her, too, but he missed. And she fell flat on her face, expecting the next bullet to get her, but he didn't fire again."

"He thought the first one did it," said Crawley.

"I don't know," said Wills. "He wasted four on the old guy."

"He hadn't expected both of them," said Levine. "She rattled him. Did he clean the register?"

"All the bills and a handful of quarters. She figures about sixty-two bucks."

"What about identification?" asked Crawley. "She saw him, right?"

"Right. But you know this kind of neighborhood. At first, she said she recognized him. Then she thought it over, and now she says she was mistaken."

Crawley made a sour sound and said, "Does she know the old man is dead?"

Wills looked surprised. "I didn't know it myself. He was alive when the ambulance got him."

"Died on the way to the hospital. Okay, let's go talk to her."

Oh, God, thought Levine. *We've got to be the ones to tell her.*

Don't think morbid thoughts. Think about life. Think about your work.

Wills stayed in front, by the door. Crawley led the way back. It was a typical slum neighborhood grocery. The store area was too narrow to begin with, both sides lined with shelves. A glass-faced enamel-sided cooler, full of cold cuts and potato salad and quarter-pound bricks of butter, ran parallel to the side shelves down the middle of the store. At one end there was a small ragged-wood counter holding the cash register and candy jars and a tilted stack of English Muffin packages. Beyond this counter were the bread and pastry shelves and, at the far end, a small frozen food chest. This row gave enough room on the customer's side for a man to turn around, if he did so carefully, and just enough room on the owner's side for a man to sidle along sideways.

Crawley led the way down the length of the store and through the dim doorway at the rear. They went through a tiny dark stock area and another doorway to the smallest and most overcrowded living room Levine had ever seen.

Mohair and tassels and gilt and lion's legs, that was the living room. Chubby hassocks and overstuffed chairs and amber lampshades and tiny intricate doilies on every flat surface. The carpet-design was twists and corkscrews, in muted dark faded colors. The wallpaper was somber, with a curling ensnarled vine pattern writhing on it. The ceiling was low. This wasn't a room, it was a warm crowded den, a little hole in the ground for frightened gray mice.

The woman sat deep within one of the overstuffed chairs. She was short and very stout, dressed in dark clothing nearly the same dull hue as the chair, so that only her pale frightened face was at first noticeable, and then the heavy pale hands twisting in her lap.

Stanton, the other uniformed patrolman, rose from the sofa, saying to the woman, "These men are detectives. They'll want to talk to you a little. Try to remember about the boy, will you? You know we won't let anything happen to you."

Crawley asked him, "The lab been here yet?"

"No, sir, not yet."

"You and Wills stick around up front till they show."

"Right." He excused himself as he edged around Levine and left.

Crawley took Stanton's former place on the sofa, and Levine worked his way among the hassocks and drum tables to the chair most distant from the light, off to the woman's left.

Crawley said, "Mrs. Kosofsky, we want to get the man who did this. We don't want to let him do it again, to somebody else."

The woman didn't move, didn't speak. Her gaze remained fixed on Crawley's lips.

Crawley said, "You told the patrolman you could identify the man who did it."

After a long second of silence, the woman trembled, shivered as through suddenly cold. She shook her head heavily from side to side, saying, "No. No, I was wrong. It was very fast, too fast. I couldn't see him good."

Levine sighed and shifted position. He knew it was useless. She wouldn't tell them anything, she would only withdraw deeper and deeper into the burrow, wanting no revenge, no return, nothing but to be left alone.

"You saw him," said Crawley, his voice loud and harsh. "You're afraid he'll get you if you talk to us, is that it?"

The woman's head was shaking again, and she repeated, "No. No. No."

"He shot a gun at you," Crawley reminded her. "Don't you want us to get him for that?"

"No. No."

"Don't you want us to get your money back?"

"No. No." She wasn't listening to Crawley, she was merely shaking her head and repeating the one word over and over again.

"Don't you want us to get the man who killed your husband?"

Levine started. He'd known that was what Crawley was leading up to, but it still shocked him. The viciousness of it cut into him, but he knew it was the only way they'd get any information from her, to hit her with the death of her husband just as hard as they could.

The woman continued to shake her head a few seconds longer, and then stopped abruptly, staring full at Crawley for the first time. "What you say?"

"The man who murdered your husband," said Crawley. "Don't you want us to get him for murdering your husband?"

"Nathan?"

"He's dead."

"No," she said, more forcefully than before, and half-rose from the chair.

"He died in the ambulance," said Crawley doggedly, "died before he got to the hospital."

Then they waited. Levine bit down hard on his lower lip, hard enough to bring blood. He knew Crawley was right, it was the only possible way. But Levine couldn't have done it. To think of death was terrible enough. To *use* death — to use the fact of it as a weapon — no, that he could never do.

The woman fell back into the seat, and her face was suddenly stark and clear in every detail. Rounded brow and narrow nose and prominent cheekbones and small chin, all covered by skin as white as candle wax, stretched taut across the skull.

Crawley took a deep breath. "He murdered your husband," he said. "Do you want him to go free?"

In the silence now they could hear vague distant sounds, people walking, talking to one another, listening to the radio or watching television, far away in another world.

At last, she spoke. "Brodek," she said. Her voice was flat. She stared at the opposite wall. "Danny Brodek. From the next block down."

"A boy?"

"Sixteen, seventeen."

Crawley would have asked more, but Levine got to his feet and said, "Thank you, Mrs. Kosofsky."

She closed her eyes.

In the phone book in the front of the store they found one Brodek—Harry R—listed with an address on Tanahee. They went out to the car and drove slowly down the next block to the building they wanted. A taxi passed them, its vacancy light lit. Nothing else moved.

This block, like the one before it and the one after it, was lined on both sides with red brick tenements, five stories high. The building they were looking for was two-thirds of the way down the block. They left the car and went inside.

In the hall, there was the smell of food. The hall was amber tile, and the doors were dark green, with metal numbers. The stairs led up abruptly to the left, midway down the hall. Opposite them were the mailboxes, warped from too much rifling.

They found the name, shakily capital-lettered on an odd scrap of paper and stuck into the mailbox marked 4-D.

Above the first floor, the walls were plaster, painted a green slightly darker than the doors. Sounds of television filtered through most of the doors. Crawley waited at the fourth floor landing for Levine to catch up. Levine climbed stairs slowly, afraid of being short of breath. When he was short of breath, the skipped heart beats became more frequent.

Crawley rapped on the door marked 4-D. Television sounds came through this one, too. After a minute, the door opened a crack, as far as it would go with the chain attached. A woman glared out at them. "What you want?"

"Police," said Crawley. "Open the door."

"What you want?" she asked again.

"Open up," said Crawley impatiently.

Levine took out his wallet, flipped it open to show the badge pinned to the ID label. "We want to talk to you for a minute," he said, trying to make his voice as gentle as possible.

The woman hesitated, then shut the door and they heard the clinking of the chain being removed. She opened the door again, releasing into the hall a smell of beer and vegetable soup. She said, "All right. Come." Turning away, she waddled down an unlit corridor toward the living room.

This room was furnished much like the den behind the grocery store, but the effect was different. It was a somewhat larger room, dominated by a blue plastic television set with a bulging screen. An automobile chase was careening across the screen, pre-war Fords and Mercuries, accompanied by frantic music.

A short heavy man in T-shirt and work pants and slippers sat on the sofa, holding a can of beer and watching the television set. Beyond him, a taller, younger version of himself, in khaki slacks and flannel shirt with the collar turned up, was watching, with a cold and wary eye, the entrance of the two policemen.

The man turned sourly, and his wife said, "They're police. They want to talk to us."

Crawley walked across the room and stood in front of the boy. "You Danny Brodek?"

"So what?"

"Get on your feet."

"Why should I?"

Before Crawley could answer, Mrs. Brodek stepped between him and her son, saying rapidly, "What you want Danny for? He ain't done nothing. He's been right here all night long."

Levine, who had waited by the corridor doorway, shook his head grimly. This was going to be just as bad as the scene with Mrs. Kosofsky. Maybe worse.

Crawley said, "He told you to say that? Did he tell you why? Did he tell you what he did tonight?"

It was the father who answered. "He didn't do nothing. You make a Federal case out of everything, you cops. Kids maybe steal a hubcap, knock out a streetlight, what the hell? They're kids."

Over Mrs. Brodek's shoulder, Crawley said to the boy, "Didn't you tell them, Danny?"

"Tell them what?"

"Do you want me to tell them?"

"I don't know what you're talking about."

On the television screen, the automobile chase was finished. A snarling character said, "I don't know what you're talking about." Another character said back, "You know what I'm talking about, Kid."

Crawley turned to Mr. Brodek. "Your boy didn't steal any hubcap tonight," he said. "He held up the grocery store in the next block. Kosofsky's."

The boy said, "You're nuts."

Mrs. Brodek said, "Not Danny. Danny wouldn't do nothing like that."

"He shot the old man," said Crawley heavily. "Shot him four times."

"Shot him!" cried Brodek. "How? Where's he going to get a gun? Answer me that, where's a young kid like that going to get a gun?"

Levine spoke up for the first time. "We don't know where they get them, Mr. Brodek," he said. "All we know is they get them. And then they use them."

"I'll tell you where when he tells us," said Crawley.

Mrs. Brodek said again, "Danny wouldn't do nothing like that. You've got it wrong."

Levine said, "Wait, Jack," to his partner. To Mrs. Brodek, he said, "Danny did it. There isn't any question. If there was a question, we wouldn't arrest him."

"The hell with that!" cried Brodek. "I know about you cops, you got these arrest quotas. You got to look good, you got to make a lot of arrests."

"If we make a lot of wrong arrests," Levine told him, trying to be patient for the sake of what this would do to Brodek when he finally had to admit the truth, "we embarrass the Police Department. If we make a lot of wrong arrests, we don't stay on the force."

Crawley said, angrily, "Danny, you aren't doing yourself any favors. And you aren't doing your parents any favors either. You want them charged with accessory? The old man died!"

In the silence, Levine said softly, "We have a witness, Mrs. Brodek, Mr. Brodek. The wife, the old man's wife. She was in the apartment behind the store and heard the shots. She ran out to the front and saw Danny at the cash register. She'll make a positive identification."

"Sure she will," said the boy.

Levine looked at him. "You killed her husband, boy. She'll identify you."

"So why didn't I bump her while I was at it?"

"You tried," said Crawley. "You fired one shot, saw her fall, and then you ran."

The boy grinned. "Yeah, that's a dandy. Think it'll hold up in court? An excitable old woman, she only saw this guy while he's shooting at her, and then he ran out. Some positive identification."

"They teach bad law on television, boy," said Levine. "It'll hold up."

"Not if I was here all night, and I was. Wasn't I, Mom?"

Defiantly, Mrs. Brodek said, "Danny didn't leave this room for a minute tonight. Not a minute."

Levine said, "Mrs. Brodek, he *killed*. Your son took a man's life. He was seen."

"She could have been mistaken. It all happened so fast, I bet she could have been mistaken. She only thought it was Danny."

"If it happened to your husband, Mrs. Brodek, would *you* make a mistake?"

Mr. Brodek said, "You don't make me believe that. I know my son. You got this wrong somewhere."

Crawley said, "Hidden in his bedroom, or hidden somewhere nearby, there's sixty-two dollars, most of it in bills, three or four dollars in quarters. And the gun's probably with it."

"That's what he committed murder for, Mr. Brodek," said Levine. "Sixty-two dollars."

"I'm going to go get it," said Crawley, turning toward the door on the other side of the living room.

Brodek jumped up, shouting, "The hell you are! Let's see your warrant! I got that much law from television, mister, you don't just come busting in here and make a search. You got to have a warrant."

Crawley looked at Levine in disgust and frustration, and Levine knew what he was thinking. The simple thing to do would be to go ahead and make the arrest and leave the Brodeks still telling their lie. That would be the simple thing to do, but it would also be the wrong thing to do. If the Brodeks were still maintaining the lie once Crawley and Levine left, they would be stuck with it. They wouldn't dare admit the truth after that, not even if they could be made to believe it.

They must be wondering already, but could not admit their doubts. If they were left alone now, they would make the search themselves that they had just kept Crawley from making, and they would find the money and the gun. The

73

money and the gun would be somewhere in Danny Brodek's bedroom. The money stuffed into the toe of a shoe in the closet, maybe. The gun under the mattress or at the bottom of a full wastebasket.

If the Brodeks found the money and the gun, and believed that they didn't dare change their story, they would get rid of the evidence. The paper money ripped up and flushed down the toilet. The quarters spent, or thrown out the window. The gun dropped down a sewer.

Without the money, without the gun, without breaking Danny Brodek's alibi, he had a better than even chance of getting away scot-free. In all probability, the grand jury wouldn't even return an indictment. The unsupported statement of an old woman, who only had a few hectic seconds for identification, against a total lack of evidence and a rock solid alibi by the boy's parents, and the case was foredoomed.

But Danny Brodek had *killed*. He had taken life, and he couldn't get away with it. Nothing else in the world, so far as Levine was concerned, was as heinous, as vivious, as *evil*, as the untimely taking of life.

Couldn't the boy himself understand what he'd done? Nathan Kosofsky was dead. He didn't exist any more. He didn't breathe, he didn't see or hear or taste or touch or smell. The pit that yawned so widely in Levine's fears had been opened for Nathan Kosofsky and he had tumbled in. Never to live, ever again.

If the boy couldn't understand the enormity of what he'd done, if he was too young, if life to him was still too natural and inevitable a gift, then surely his parents were old enough to understand. Did Mr. Brodek never lie awake in bed and wonder at the frail and transient sound of his own heart pumping the life through his veins? Had Mrs. Brodek not felt the cringing closeness of the fear of death when she was about to give birth to her son? They knew, they had to know, what murder really meant.

He wanted to ask them, or to remind them, but the awful truths swirling in his brain wouldn't solidify into words and sentences. There is no real way to phrase an emotion.

Crawley, across the room, sighed heavily and said, "Okay. You'll set your own parents up for the bad one. That's okay. We've got the eye-witness. And there'll be more; a fingerprint on the cash register, somebody who saw you run out of the store —— "

No one had seen Danny Brodek run from the store. Looking at the smug young face, Levine knew there would be no fingerprints on the cash register. It's just as easy to knuckle the No Sale key to open the cash drawer.

He said, to the boy's father, "On the way out of the store, Danny was mad and scared and nervous. He pulled the door open, and the bell over it rang. He took out his anger and his nervousness on it, yanking the bell down. We'll find that somewhere between here and the store, and there may be prints on it. There also may be scratches on his hand, from yanking the bell mechanism off the door frame."

Quickly, Danny said, "Lots of people got scratches on their hands. I was playing with a cat this afternoon, coming home from school. He gave me a couple scratches. See?" He held out his right hand, with three pink ragged tears across the surface of the palm.

Crawley said, "I've played with cats, too, kid. I always got my scratches on the back of my hand."

The boy shrugged. The statement needed no answer.

Crawley went on, "You played with this cat a long while, huh? Long enough to get three scratches, is that it?"

"That's it. Prove different."

"Let's see the scratches on your left hand."

The boy allowed tension to show for just an instant, before he said, "I don't have any on my left hand. Just the right. So what?"

Crawley turned to the father. "Does that sound right to you?"

"Why not?" demanded Brodek defensively. "You play with a cat, maybe you only use one hand. You trying to railroad my son because of some cat scratches?"

This wasn't the way to do it, and Levine knew it. Little corroborative proofs, they weren't enough. They could add weight to an already-held conviction, that's all they could do. They couldn't change an opposite conviction.

The Brodeks had to be reminded, some way, of the enormity of what their son had done. Levine wished he could open his brain for them like a book, so they could look in and read it there. They must know, they must at their ages have some inkling of the monstrousness of death. But they had to be reminded.

There was one way to do it. Levine knew the way, and shrank from it. It was as necessary as Crawley's brutality with the old woman in the back of the store. Just as necessary. But more brutal. And he had flinched away from that earlier, lesser brutality, telling himself *he* could never do such a thing.

He looked over at his partner, hoping Crawley would think of the way, hoping Crawley would take the action from Levine. But Crawley was still parading his little corroborative proofs, before an audience not yet prepared to accept them.

Levine shook his head, and took a deep breath, and stepped forward an additional pace into the room. He said, "May I use your phone?"

They all looked at him, Crawley puzzled, the boy wary, the parents hostile. The father finally shrugged and said, "Why not? On the stand there, by the TV."

"May I turn the volume down?"

"Turn the damn thing off if you want, who can pay any attention to it?"

"Thank you."

Levine switched off the television set, then searched in the phone book and found the number of Kosofsky's Grocery.

He dialed, and a male voice answered on the first ring, saying, "Kosofsky's. Hello?"

"Is this Stanton?"

"No, Wills. Who's this?"

"Detective Levine. I was down there a little while ago."

"Oh, sure. What can I do for you, sir?"

"How's Mrs. Kosofsky now?"

"How is she? I don't know. I mean, she isn't hysterical or anything. She's just sitting there."

"Is she capable of going for a walk?"

Wills', "I guess so," was drowned out by Mr. Brodek's shouted, "What the hell are you up to?"

Into the phone, Levine said, "Hold on a second." He cupped his hand over the mouthpiece, and looked at the angry father. "I want you to understand," he told him, "just what it was your son did tonight. I want to make sure you understand. So I'm going to have Mrs. Kosofsky come up here. For her to look at Danny again. And for you to look at her while she's looking at him."

Brodek paled slightly, and an uncertain look came into his eyes. He glanced quickly at his son, then even more quickly back at Levine. "The hell with you," he said defiantly. "Danny was here all night. Do whatever the hell you want."

Mrs. Brodek started to speak, but cut it off at the outset, making only a tiny sound in her throat. But it was enough to make the rest swivel their heads and look at her. Her eyes were wide. Strain lines had deepened around her mouth, and one hand trembled at the base of her throat. She stared in mute appeal at Levine, her eyes clearly saying, *Don't make me know.*

Levine forced himself to turn away, say into the phone, "I'm at the Brodeks. Bring Mrs. Kosofsky up here, will you? It's the next block down to your right, 1342, apartment 4-D."

It was a long silent wait. No one spoke at all from the time Levine hung up the telephone till the time Wills arrived with

Mrs. Kosofsky. The five of them sat in the drab living room, avoiding one another's eyes. From another room, deeper in the apartment, a clock that had before been unnoticeable now ticked loudly. The ticks were very fast, but the minutes they clocked off crept slowly by.

When the rapping finally came at the hall door, they all jumped. Mrs. Brodek turned her hopeless eyes toward Levine again, but he looked away, at his partner. Crawley lumbered to his feet and out of the room, down the corridor to the front door. Those in the room heard him open the door, heard the murmur of male voices, and then the clear frightened voice of the old woman: "Who lives here? Who lives in this place?"

Levine looked up and saw that Danny Brodek was watching him, eyes hard and cold, face set in lines of bitter hatred. Levine held his gaze, pitying him, until Danny looked away, mouth twisting in an expression of scorn that didn't quite come off.

Then Crawley came back into the room, stepping aside for the old woman to follow him in. Beyond her could be seen the pale young face of the patrolman, Wills.

She saw Levine first. Her eyes were frightened and bewildered. Her fingers plucked at a button of the long black coat she now wore over her dress. In the brighter light of this room, she looked older, weaker, more helpless.

She looked second at Mrs. Brodek, whose expression was as terrified as her own, and then she saw Danny.

She cried out, a high-pitched failing whimper, and turned hurriedly away, pushing against Wills, jabbering, "Away! Away! I go away!"

Levine's voice sounded over her hysteria: "It's okay, Wills. Help her back to the store." He couldn't keep the bitter rage from his voice. The others might have thought it was rage against Danny Brodek, but they would have been wrong. It was rage against himself. What good would it do to convict Danny Brodek, to jail him for twenty or thirty years? Would it undo what he had done? Would it restore her husband to Mrs. Kosofsky? It wouldn't. But nothing less could excuse the vicious thing he had just done to her.

Faltering, nearly whispering, Mrs. Brodek said, "I want to talk to Danny. I want to talk to my son."

Her husband glared warningly at her. "Esther, he was here all —— "

"I want to talk to my son!"

Levine said, "All right." Down the corridor, the door snicked shut behind Wills and the old woman.

Mrs. Brodek said, "Alone. In his bedroom."

Levine looked at Crawley, who shrugged and said, "Three minutes. Then we come in."

The boy said, "Mom, what's there to talk about?"

"I want to talk to you," she told him icily. "Now."

She led the way from the room, Danny Brodek following her reluctantly, pausing to throw back one poisonous glance at Levine before shutting the connecting door.

Brodek cleared his throat, looking uncertainly at the two detectives. "Well," he said. "Well. She really — she really thinks it was him, doesn't she?"

"She sure does," said Crawley.

Brodek shook his head slowly. "Not Danny," he said, but he was talking to himself.

Then they heard Mrs. Brodek cry out from the bedroom, and a muffled thump. All three men dashed across the living room, Crawley reaching the door first and throwing it open, leading the way down the short hall to the second door and running inside. Levine followed him, and Brodek, grunting, "My God. Oh, my God," came in third.

Mrs. Brodek sat hunched on the floor of the tiny bedroom, arms folded on the seat of an unpainted kitchen chair. A bright-colored shirt was hung askew on the back of the chair.

She looked up as they ran in, and her face was a blank, drained of all emotion and all life and all personality. In a voice as toneless and blank as her face, she told him, "He went up the fire escape. He got the gun, from under his mattress. He went up the fire escape."

Brodek started toward the open window, but Crawley pulled him back, saying, "He might be waiting up there. He'll fire at the first head he sees."

Levine had found a comic book and a small gray cap on the dresser-top. He twisted the comic book in a large cylinder, stuck the cap on top of it, held it slowly and cautiously out the window. From above, silhouetted, it would look like a head and neck.

The shot rang loud from above, and the comic book was jerked from Levine's hand. He pulled his hand back and Crawley said, "The stairs."

Levine followed his partner back out of the bedroom. The last he saw in there, Mr. Brodek was reaching down, with an awkward shyness, to touch his wife's cheek.

This was the top floor of the building. After this, the staircase went up one more flight, ending at a metal-faced door which opened onto the roof. Crawley led the way, his small flat pistol now in his hand, and Levine climbed more slowly after him.

He got midway up the flight before Crawley pushed open the door, stepped cautiously out onto the roof, and the single shot snapped out. Crawley doubled suddenly, stepping involuntarily back, and would have fallen backward down the stairs if Levine hadn't reached him in time and struggled him to a half-sitting position, wedged between the top step and the wall.

Crawley's face was gray, his mouth strained white. "From the right," he said, his voice low and bitter. "Down low, I saw the flash."

"Where?" Levine asked him. "Where did he get you?"

"Leg. Right leg, high up. Just the fat, I think."

From outside, they could hear a man's voice braying,

"Danny! Danny! For God's sake, Danny!" It was Mr. Brodek, shouting up from the bedroom window.

"Get the light," whispered Crawley.

Not until then had Levine realized how rattled he'd been just now. Twenty-four years on the force. When did you become a professional? How?

He straightened up, reaching up to the bare bulb in its socket high on the wall near the door. The bulb burned his fingers, but it took only the one turn to put it out.

Light still filtered up from the floor below, but no longer enough to keep him from making out shapes on the roof. He crouched over Crawley, blinking until his eyes got used to the darkness.

To the right, curving over the top of the knee-high wall around the roof, were the top bars of the fire escape. Black shadow at the base of the wall, all around. The boy was low, lying prone against the wall in the darkness, where he couldn't be seen.

"I can see the fire escape from here," muttered Crawley. " I've got him boxed. Go on down to the car and call for help."

"Right," said Levine.

He had just turned away when Crawley grabbed his arm. "No. Listen!"

He listened. Soft scrapings, outside and to the right. A sudden flurry of footsteps, running, receding.

"Over the roofs!" cried Crawley. "*Damn* this leg! Go after him!"

"Ambulance," said Levine.

"Go *after* him! *They* can make the call." He motioned at the foot of the stairs, and Levine, turning, saw down there anxious, frightened, bewildered faces peering up, bodies clothed in robes and slippers.

"*Go on!*" cried Crawley.

Levine moved, jumping out onto the roof in a half-crouch,

ducking away to the right. The revolver was in his hand, his eyes were staring into the darkness.

Three rooftops away, he saw the flash of white, the boy's shirt. Levine ran after him.

Across the first roof, he ran with mouth open, but his throat dried and constricted, and across the second roof he ran with his mouth shut, trying to swallow. But he couldn't get enough air in through his nostrils, and after that he alternated, mouth open and mouth closed, looking like a frantic fish, running like a comic fat man, clambering over the intervening knee-high walls with painful slowness.

There were seven rooftops to the corner, and the corner building was only three stories high. The boy hesitated, dashed one way and then the other, and Levine was catching up. Then the boy turned, fired wildly at him, and raced to the fire escape. He was young and lithe, slender. His legs went over the side, his body slid down; the last thing Levine saw of him was the white face.

Two more roofs. Levine stumbled across them, and he no longer needed the heel of his hand to his ear in order to hear his heart. He could hear it plainly, over the rush of his breathing, a brushlike throb — throb — throb — throb — throb —

Every six or seven beats.

He got to the fire escape, winded, and looked over. Five flights down, a long dizzying way, to the blackness of the bottom. He saw a flash of the boy in motion, two flights down. "Stop!" he cried, knowing it was useless.

He climbed over onto the rungs, heavy and cumbersome. His revolver clanged against the top rung as he descended and, as if in answer, the boy's gun clanged against metal down below.

The first flight down was a metal ladder, and after that narrow steep metal staircases with a landing at every floor. He plummeted down, never quite on balance, the boy always two flights ahead.

At the second floor, he paused, looked over the side, saw the boy drop lightly to the ground, turn back toward the building, heard the grate of door hinges not used to opening.

The basement. And the flashlight was in the glove compartment of the squad car. Crawley had a pencil flash, six buildings and three floors away.

Levine moved again, hurrying as fast as before. At the bottom, there was a jump. He hung by his hands, the revolver digging into his palm, and dropped, feeling it hard in his ankles.

The back of the building was dark, with a darker rectangle in it, and fire flashed in that rectangle. Something tugged at Levine's sleeve, at the elbow. He ducked to the right, ran forward, and was in the basement.

Ahead of him, something toppled over with a wooden crash, and the boy cursed. Levine used the noise to move deeper into the basement, to the right, so he couldn't be outlined against the doorway, which was a gray hole now in a world suddenly black. He came up against a wall, rough brick and bits of plaster, and stopped, breathing hard, trying to breathe silently and to listen.

He wanted to listen for sounds of the boy, but the rhythmic pounding of his heart was too loud, too pervasive. He had to hear it out first, to count it, and to know that now it was skipping every sixth beat. His breath burned in his lungs, a metal band was constricted about his chest, his head felt hot and heavy and fuzzy. There were blue sparks at the corners of his vision.

There was another clatter from deeper inside the basement, to the left, and the faint sound of a doorknob being turned, turned back, turned again.

Levine cleared his throat. When he spoke, he expected his voice to be high-pitched, but it wasn't. It was as deep and as strong as normal, maybe even a little deeper and a little louder. "It's locked, Danny," he said. "Give it up. Throw the gun out the doorway."

The reply was another fire-flash, and an echoing thunder-clap, too loud for the small bare-walled room they were in. And, after it, the whining ricochet as the bullet went wide.

That's the third time, thought Levine. *The third time he's given me a target, and I haven't shot at him. I could have shot at the flash, this time or the last. I could have shot at him on the roof, when he stood still just before going down the fire escape.*

Aloud, he said, "That won't do you any good, Danny. You can't hit a voice. Give it up, prowl cars are converging here from all over Brooklyn."

"I'll be long gone," said the sudden voice, and it was surprisingly close, surprisingly loud.

"You can't get out the door without me seeing you," Levine told him. "Give it up."

"I can see you, cop," said the young voice. "You can't see me, but I can see you."

Levine knew it was a lie. Otherwise, the boy would have shot him down before this. He said, "It won't go so bad for you, Danny, if you give up now. You're young, you'll get a lighter sentence. How old are you? Sixteen, isn't it?"

"I'm going to gun you down, cop," said the boy's voice. It seemed to be closer, moving to Levine's right. The boy was trying to get behind him, get Levine between himself and the doorway, so he'd have a silhouette to aim at.

Levine slid cautiously along the wall, feeling his way. "You aren't going to gun anybody down," he said into the darkness. "Not anybody else."

Another flash, another thunderclap, and the shatter of glass behind him. The voice said, "You don't even have a gun on you."

"I don't shoot at shadows, Danny. Or old men."

"*I* do, old man."

How old is he? wondered Levine. *Sixteen, probably. Thirty-seven years younger than me.*

"You're afraid," taunted the voice, weaving closer. "You ought to run, cop, but you're afraid."

I am, thought Levine. *I am, but not for the reason you think.*

It was true. From the minute he'd ducked into this basement room, Levine had stopped being afraid of his own death at the hands of this boy. He was fifty-three years of age. If anything was going to get him tonight it was going to be that heart of his, skipping now on number five. It wasn't going to be the boy, except indirectly, because of the heart.

But he *was* afraid. He was afraid of the revolver in his own hand, the feel of the trigger, and the knowledge that he had let three chances go by. He was afraid of his job, because his job said he was supposed to bring this boy down. Kill him or wound him, but bring him down.

Thirty-seven years. That was what separated them, thirty-seven years of life. Why should it be up to *him* to steal those thirty-seven years from this boy? Why should *he* have to be the one?

"You're a goner, cop," said the voice. "You're a dead man. I'm coming in on you."

It didn't matter what Danny Brodek had done. It didn't matter about Nathan Kosofsky, who was dead. An eye for an eye, a life for a life. No! A destroyed life could not be restored by more destruction of life.

I can't do it, Levine thought. *I can't do it to him.*

He said, "Danny, you're wrong. Listen to me, for God's sake, you're wrong."

"You better run, cop," crooned the voice. "You better hurry."

Levine heard the boy, soft slow sounds closer to his left, weaving slowly nearer. "I don't *want* to kill you, Danny!" he cried. "Can't you understand that? I don't *want* to kill you!"

"I want to kill *you,* cop," whispered the voice.

"Don't you know what dying is?" pleaded Levine. He had his hand out now in a begging gesture, though the boy couldn't see him. "Don't you know what it means to die? To stop, like a watch. Never to see anything any more, never to hear or touch or know anything any more. Never to *be* any more."

"That's the way it's going to be, cop," soothed the young voice. Very close now, very close.

He was too young. Levine knew it, knew the boy was too young to *feel* what death really is. He was too young to know what he wanted to take from Levine, what Levine didn't want to take from him.

Every fourth beat.

Thirty-seven years.

"You're a dead man, cop," breathed the young voice, directly in front of him.

And light dazzled them both.

It all happened so fast. One second, they were doing their dance of death here together, alone, just the two of them in all the world. The next second, the flashlight beam hit them both, the clumsy uniformed patrolman was standing in the doorway, saying, "Hey!" Making himself a target, and the boy, slender, turning like a snake, his eyes glinting in the light, the gun swinging around at the light and the figure behind the light.

Levine's heart stopped, one beat.

And every muscle, every nerve, every *bone* in his body tensed and tightened and drew in on itself, squeezing him shut, and the sound of the revolver going off slammed into him, pounding his stomach.

The boy screamed, hurtling down out of the light, the gun clattering away from his fingers.

"Jesus God have mercy!" breathed the patrolman. It was Wills. He came on in, unsteadily, the flashlight trembling in his hand as he pointed its beam at the boy crumpled on the floor.

Levine looked down at himself and saw the thin trail of blue-gray smoke rising up from the barrel of his revolver. Saw his hands still tensed shut into claws, into fists, the first finger of his right hand still squeezing the trigger back against its guard.

He willed his hands open, and the revolver fell to the floor.

Wills went down on one knee beside the boy. After a minute, he straightened, saying, "Dead. Right through the heart, I guess."

Levine sagged against the wall. His mouth hung open. He couldn't seem to close it.

Wills said, "What's the matter? You okay?"

With an effort, Levine nodded his head. "I'm okay," he said. "Call in. Go on, call in."

"Well. I'll be right back."

Wills left, and Levine looked down at the new young death. His eyes saw the colors of the floor, the walls, the clothing on the corpse. His shoulders felt the weight of his overcoat. His ears heard the receding footsteps of the young patrolman. His nose smelled the sharp tang of recent gunfire. His mouth tasted the briny after-effect of fear.

"I'm sorry," he whispered.

THE SOUND OF MURDER

Detective Abraham Levine of Brooklyn's Forty-Third Precinct sat at his desk in the squadroom and longed for a cigarette. The fingers of his left hand kept closing and clenching, feeling awkward without the paper-rolled tube of tobacco. He held a pencil for a while but unconsciously brought it to his mouth. He didn't realize what he was doing till he tasted the gritty staleness of the eraser. Then he put the pencil away in a drawer, and tried unsuccessfully to concentrate on the national news in the news magazine.

The world conspired against a man who tried to give up smoking. All around him were other people puffing ciragettes casually and unconcernedly, not making any fuss about it at all, making by their very nonchalance his own grim reasons for giving them up seem silly and hyper-sensitive. If he isolated himself from other smokers with the aid of television or radio, the cigarette commercials with their erotic smoking and their catchy jingles would surely drive him mad. Also, he would find that the most frequent sentence in popular fiction was, "He lit another cigarette." Statesmen and entertainers seemed inevitably to be smoking whenever news photographers snapped them for posterity, and even the news items were against him: He had just reread for the third time an announcement to the world that Pope John XXIII was the first Prelate of the Roman Catholic Church to smoke cigarettes in public.

Levine closed the magazine in irritation, and from the cover smiled at him the Governor of a midwestern state, cigarette in F.D.R. cigarette-holder at a jaunty angle in his mouth. Levine closed his eyes, saddened by the knowledge that he had turned himself at this late date into a comic character. A grown man who tries to give up smoking *is* comic, a Robert Benchley or a W.C. Fields, bumbling along, plagued by trivia, his life an endless gauntlet of minor crises. *They could do a one-reeler on me,* Levine thought. *A great little comedy. Laurel without Hardy. Because Hardy died of a heart attack.*

Abraham Levine, at fifty-three years of age, was twenty-four years a cop and eight years into the heart-attack range. When he went to bed at night, he kept himself awake by listening to the silence that replaced every eighth or ninth beat of his heart. When he had to climb stairs or lift anything heavy, he was acutely conscious of the labored heaviness of his breathing and of the way those missed heartbeats came closer and closer together, every seventh beat and then every sixth and then every fifth —

Some day, he knew, his heart would skip two beats in a row, and on that day Abraham Levine would stop, because there wouldn't be any third beat. None at all, not ever.

Four months ago, he'd gone to the doctor, and the doctor had checked him over very carefully, and he had submitted to it feeling like an aging auto brought to a mechanic by an owner who wanted to know whether it was worth while to fix the old boat up or should he just junk the thing and get another. (In the house next door to his, a baby cried every night lately. The new model, crying for the old and the obsolete to get off the road.)

So he'd gone to the doctor, and the doctor had told him not to worry. He had that little skip in his heartbeat, but that wasn't anything dangerous, lots of people had that. And his blood pressure was a little high, but not much, not enough to concern himself about. So the doctor told him he was healthy, and collected his fee, and Levine left, unconvinced.

So when he went back again three days ago, still frightened by the skip and the shortness of breath and the occasional chest cramps when he was excited or afraid, the doctor had told him the same things all over again, and had added, "If you really want to do something for that heart of yours, you can give up smoking."

He hadn't had a cigarette since, and for the first time in his life he was beginning really to understand the wails of the arrested junkies, locked away in a cell with nothing to ease their craving. He was beginning to be ashamed of himself, for having become so completely dependent on something so useless and so harmful. Three days now. Comic or not, he was going to make it.

Opening his eyes, he glared at the cigarette-smoking Governor and shoved the magazine into a drawer. Then he looked around the squadroom, empty except for himself and his partner, Crawley, sitting over there smoking contentedly at his desk by the filing cabinet as he worked on a report. Rizzo and McFarlane, the other two detectives on this shift, were out on a call but would probably be back soon. Levine longed for the phone to ring, for something to happen to distract him, to keep mind and hands occupied and forgetful of cigarettes. He looked around the room, at a loss, and his left hand clenched and closed on the desk, lonely and incomplete.

When the rapping came at the door, it was so faint that Levine barely heard it, and Crawley didn't even look up.

But any sound at all would have attracted Levine's straining attention. He looked over, saw a foreshortened shadow against the frosted glass of the door, and called, "Come in."

Crawley looked up. "What?"

"Someone at the door." Levine called out again, and this time the doorknob hesitantly turned, and a child walked in.

It was a little girl of about ten, in a frilly frock of pale pink, with a flared skirt, with gold-buckled black shoes and ribbed white socks. Her hair was pale blonde, combed and brushed and shampooed to gleaming cleanliness, brushed back from her forehead and held by a pink bow atop her head, then cascading straight down her back nearly to her waist. Her eyes were huge and bright blue, her face a creamy oval. She was a little girl in an ad for children's clothing in the *Sunday Times*. She was a story illustration in *Ladies' Home Journal*. She was . Alice in Blunderland, gazing with wide-eyed curious innocence into the bullpen, the squadroom, the home and office of the detectives of the Forty-Third Precinct, the men whose job it was to catch the stupid and the nasty so that other men could punish them.

She saw, looking into this brutal room, two men and a lot of old furniture.

It was inevitably to Levine that the little girl spoke: "May I come in?" Her voice was as faint as her tapping on the door had been. She was poised to flee at the first loud noise.

Levine automatically lowered his own voice when he answered. "Of course. Come on in. Sit over here." He motioned at the straight-backed wooden chair beside his desk.

The girl crossed the threshold, carefully closed the door again behind her, and came on silent feet across the room, glancing sidelong at Crawley, then establishing herself on the edge of the chair, her toes touching the floor, still ready for flight at any second. She studied Levine. "I want to talk to a detective," she said. "Are you a detective?"

Levine nodded. "Yes, I am."

"My name," she told him solemnly, "is Amy Thornbridge Walker. I live at 717 Prospect Park West, apartment 4-A. I want to report a murder, a quite recent murder."

"A murder?"

"My mother," she said, just as solemnly, "murdered my stepfather."

Levine glanced over at Crawley, who screwed his face up in an expression meant to say, "She's a nut. Hear her out, and then she'll go home. What else can you do?"

There was nothing else he could do. He looked at Amy Thornbridge Walker again. "Tell me about it," he said. "When did it happen?"

"Two weeks ago Thursday," she said. "November 27th. At two-thirty P.M."

Her earnest calm called for belief. But children with wild stories were not unknown to the precinct. Children came in with reports of dead bodies in alleys, flying saucers on rooftops, counterfeiters in basement apartments, kidnappers in black trucks—And once out of a thousand times what the child reported was real and not the product of a young imagination on a spree. More to save the little girl's feelings than for any other reason, therefore, Levine drew to him a pencil and a sheet of paper and took down what she told him. He said, "What's your mother's name?"

"Gloria Thornbridge Walker," she said. "And my stepfather was Albert Walker. He was an attorney."

To the side, Crawley was smiling faintly at the girl's conscious formality. Levine solemnly wrote down the names, and said, "Was your father's name Thornbridge, is that it?"

"Yes. Jason Thornbridge. He died when I was very small. I think my mother killed him, too, but I'm not absolutely sure."

"I see. But you *are* absolutely sure that your mother killed Albert Walker."

"My stepfather. Yes. My first father was supposed to have

drowned by accident in Lake Champlain, which I consider very unlikely, as he was an excellent swimmer."

Levine reached into his shirt pocket, found no cigarettes there, and suddenly realized what he was doing. Irritation washed over him, but he carefully kept it from showing in his face or voice as he said, "How long have you thought that your mother killed your rea — your first father?"

"I'd never thought about it at all," she said, "until she murdered my stepfather. Naturally, I then started thinking about it."

Crawley coughed, and lit a fresh cigarette, keeping his hands up in front of his mouth. Levine said, "Did he die of drowning, too?"

"No. My stepfather wasn't athletic at all. In fact, he was nearly an invalid for the last six months of his life."

"Then how did your mother kill him?"

"She made a loud noise at him," she said calmly.

Levine's pencil stopped its motion. He looked at her searchingly, but found no trace of humor in her eyes or mouth. If she had come up here as a joke — on a bet, say from her schoolmates — then she was a fine little actress, for no sign of the joke was on her face at all.

Though how could he really tell? Levine, a childless man with a barren wife, had found it difficult over the years to communicate with the very young. A part of it, of course, was an envy he couldn't help, in the knowledge that these children could run and play with no frightening shortness of breath or tightness of chest, that they could sleep at night in their beds with no thought for the dull thudding of their hearts, that they would be alive and knowing for years and decades, for *decades,* after he himself had ceased to exist.

Before he could formulate an answer to what she'd said, the little girl jounced off the chair with the graceful gracelessness of the young and said, "I can't stay any longer. I stopped here on my way home from school. If my mother found out that I knew, and that I had told the police, she might try to murder me, too." She turned all at once and studied Crawley severely. "I am not a silly little girl," she told him. "And I am not telling a lie or making a joke. My mother murdered my stepfather, and I came in here and reported it. That's what I'm supposed to do. You aren't supposed to believe me right away, but you are supposed to investigate and find out whether or not I've told you the truth. And I have told you the truth." She turned suddenly back to Levine, an angry little girl — no, not angry, *definite* — a definite little girl filled with stern formality and a child's sense of rightness and duty. "My stepfather," she said, "was a very good man. My mother is a bad woman. You find out what she did, and punish her." She nodded briefly, as though to punctuate what she'd said, and marched to the door, reaching it as Rizzo and McFarlane came in. They looked down at her in surprise, and she stepped past them and out to the hall, closing the door after her.

Rizzo looked at Levine and jerked his thumb at the door. "What was that?"

It was Crawley who answered. "She came in to report a murder," he said. "Her Mommy killed her Daddy by making a great big noise at him."

Rizzo frowned. "Come again?"

"I'll check it out," said Levine. Not believing the girl's story, he still felt the impact of her demand on him that he do his duty. All it would take was a few phone calls. While Crawley recounted the episode at great length to Rizzo, and McFarlane took up his favorite squadroom position, seated at his desk with the chair canted back and his feet atop the desk, Levine picked up his phone and dialed the *New York Times*. He identified himself and said what he wanted, was connected to the right department, and after a few minutes the November 28th obituary notice on Albert Walker was read to him. Cause of death: a heart attack. Mortician: Junius Merriman. An even briefer call to Merriman gave him the name of Albert Walker's doctor, Henry Sheffield.

Levine thanked Merriman, assured him there was no problem, and got out the Brooklyn yellow pages to find Sheffield's number. He dialed, spoke to a nurse, and finally got Sheffield.

"I can't understand," Sheffield told him, "why the police would be interested in the case. It was heart failure, pure and simple. What seems to be the problem?"

"There's no problem," Levine told him. "Just checking it out. Was this a sudden attack? Had he had any heart trouble before?"

"Yes, he'd suffered a coronary attack about seven months ago. The second attack was more severe, and he hadn't really recovered as yet from the first. There certainly wasn't anything else to it, if that's what you're getting at."

"I didn't mean to imply anything like that," said Levine. "By the way, were you Mrs. Walker's first husband's doctor, too?"

"No, I wasn't. His name was Thornbridge, wasn't it? I never met the man. Is there some sort of question about him?"

"No, not at all." Levine evaded a few more questions, then hung up, his duty done. He turned to Crawley and shook his head. "Nothing to — "

A sudden crash behind him froze the words in his throat. He halfrose from the chair, mouth wide open, face paling as the blood rushed from his head, his nerves and muscles stiff and tingling.

It was over in a second, and he sank back into the chair, turning around to see what had happened. McFarlane was sheepishly picking himself up from the floor, his chair lying on its back beside him. He grinned shakily at Levine. "Leaned back too far that time," he said.

"Don't do that," said Levine, his voice shaky. He touched the back of his hand to his forehead, feeling cold perspiration slick against the skin. He was trembling all over. Once again, he reached to his shirt pocket for a cigarette, and this time felt an instant of panic when he found the pocket empty. He pressed the palm of his hand to the pocket, and beneath pocket and skin he felt the thrumming of his heart, and automatically counted the beats. Thum, thum, *skip,* thum, thum, thum, thum, thum, *skip,* thum, thum, ——

On the sixth beat, the *sixth* beat. He sat there listening, hand pressed to his chest, and gradually the agitation subsided and the skip came every seventh beat and then every eighth beat, and then he could dare to move again.

He licked his lips, needing a cigarette now more than at any other time in the last three days, more than he could ever remember needing a cigarette at any time in his whole life.

His resolve crumbled. Shamefacedly, he turned to his partner. "Jack, do you have a cigarette?"

Crawley looked away from McFarlane, who was checking himself for damage. "I thought you were giving them up, Abe," he said.

"Not around here. Please, Jack."

"Sure." Crawley tossed him his pack.

Levine caught the pack, shook out one cigarette, threw the rest back to Crawley. He took a book of matches from the desk drawer, put the cigarette in his mouth, feeling the comforting familiarity of it between his lips, and struck a match. He held the match up, then sat looking at the flame, struck by a sudden thought.

Albert Walker had died of a heart attack. "She made a loud noise at him." "The second attack was more severe, and he hadn't really recovered as yet from the first."

He shook the match out, took the cigarette from between his lips. It had been every sixth beat there for a while, after the loud noise of McFarlane's backward dive.

Had Gloria Thornbridge Walker *really* killed Albert Walker?

Would Abraham Levine *really* kill Abraham Levine?

The second question was easier to answer. Levine opened

the desk drawer and dropped the cigarette and matches into it.

The first question he didn't try to answer at all. He would sleep on it. Right now, he wasn't thinking straight enough.

At dinner that night, he talked it over with his wife. "Peg," he said, "I've got a problem."

"A problem?" She looked up in surprise, a short solid stout woman three years her husband's junior, her iron-gray hair rigidly curled in a home permanent. "If you're coming to me," she said, "it must be awful."

He smiled, nodding. "It is." It was rare for him to talk about his job with his wife. The younger men, he knew, discussed their work with their wives as a matter of course, expecting and receiving suggestions and ideas and advice. But he was a product of an older upbringing, and still believed instinctively that women should be shielded from the more brutal aspects of life. It was only when the problem was one he couldn't discuss with Crawley that he turned to Peg for someone to talk to. "I'm getting old," he said suddenly, thinking of the differences between himself and the younger men.

She laughed. "That's your problem? Don't feel lonely, Abe, it happens to all kinds of people. Have some more gravy."

"Let me tell you," he said. "A little girl came in today, maybe ten years old, dressed nicely, polite, very intelligent. She wanted to report that her mother had killed her stepfather."

"A little girl?" She sounded shocked. She too believed that there were those who should be shielded from the more brutal aspects of life, but with her the shielded ones were children. "A little girl? A thing like that?"

"Wait," he said. "Let me tell you. I called the doctor and he said it was a heart attack. The stepfather — Mr. Walker —

he'd had one attack already, and the second one on top of it killed him."

"But the little girl blames the mother?" Peg leaned forward. "Psychological, you think?"

"I don't know. I asked her how her mother had done the killing, and she said her mother made a loud noise at her father."

"A joke." She shook her head. "These children today, I don't know where they get their ideas. All this on the TV — "

"Maybe," he said. "I don't know. A man with a bad heart, bedridden, an invalid. A sudden shock, a loud noise, it might do it, bring on that second attack."

"What else did this little girl say?"

"That's all. Her stepfather was good, and her mother was bad, and she'd stopped off on her way home from school. She only had a minute, because she didn't want her mother to know what she was doing."

"You let her go? You didn't question her?"

Levine shrugged. "I didn't believe her," he said. "You know the imagination children have."

"But now?"

"Now, I don't know." He held up his hand, two fingers extended. "Now," he said, "there's two questions in my mind. First, is the little girl right or wrong? Did her mother actually make a loud noise that killed her stepfather or not? And if she did, then question number two: Did she do it on purpose, or was it an accident?" He waggled the two fingers and looked at his wife. "Do you see? Maybe the little girl is right, and her mother actually did cause the death, but not intentionally. If so, I don't want to make things worse for the mother by dragging it into the open. Maybe the little girl is wrong altogether, and if so it would be best to just let the whole thing slide. But maybe she's right, and it *was* murder, and then that child is in danger, because if I don't do anything, she'll try some other way, and the mother will find out."

Peg shook her head. "I don't like that, a little girl like that. Could she defend herself? A woman to kill her husband, a woman like that could kill her child just as easy. I don't like that at all, Abe."

"Neither do I." He reached for the coffee cup, drank. "The question is, what do I do?"

She shook her head again. "A child like that," she said. "A woman like that. And then again, maybe not." She looked at her husband. "For right now," she said, "you eat. We can think about it."

For the rest of dinner they discussed other things. After the meal, as usual, the craving for a cigarette suddenly intensified, and he was unable to concentrate on anything but his resolution. They watched television during the evening, and by bedtime he still hadn't made a decision. Getting ready for bed, Peg suddenly said, "The little girl. You've been thinking?"

"I'll sleep on it," he said. "Maybe in the morning. Peg, I am longing for a cigarette."

"Nails in your coffin," she said bluntly. He blinked, and went away silently to brush his teeth.

The lights turned out, they lay together in the double bed which now, with age, had a pronounced sag toward the middle, rolling them together. But it was a cold night out, a good night to lie close together and feel the warmth of life. Levine closed his eyes and drifted slowly toward sleep.

A sudden sound shook him awake. He blinked rapidly, staring up in the darkness at the ceiling, startled, disoriented, not knowing what it was. But then the sound came again, and he exhaled, releasing held breath. It was the baby from next door, crying.

Move over, world, and give us room, he thought, giving words to the baby's cries. *Make way for the new.*

And they're right, he thought. *We've got to take care of them, and guide them, and then make way for them. They're absolutely right.*

I've got to do something for that little girl, he thought.

In the morning, Levine talked to Crawley. He sat in the client's chair, beside Crawley's desk. "About that little girl," he said.

"You, too? I got to thinking about it myself, last night."

"We ought to check it out," Levine told him.

"I know. I figure I ought to look up the death of the first father. Jason Thornbridge, wasn't it?"

"Good," said Levine. "I was thinking of going to her school, talking to the teacher. If she's the kind of child who makes up wild stories all the time, then that's that, you know what I mean?"

"Sure. You know what school she's in?"

"Lathmore Elementary, over on Third."

Crawley frowned, trying to remember. "She tell you that? I didn't hear it if she did."

"No, she didn't. But it's the only one it could be." Levine grinned sheepishly. "I'm pulling a Sherlock Holmes," he said. "She told us she'd stopped in on her way home from school. So she was walking home, and there's only three schools in the right direction — so we'd be between them and Prospect Park — but they're close enough for her to walk." He checked them off on his fingers. "There's St. Aloysius, but she wasn't in a school uniform. There's PS 118, but with a Prospect Park West address and the clothing she was wearing and her good manners, she doesn't attend any public school. So that leaves Lathmore."

"Okay, Sherlock," said Crawley. "You go talk to the nice people at Lathmore. I'll dig into the Thornbridge thing."

"One of us," Levine told him, "ought to check this out with the Lieutenant first. Tell him what we want to do."

"Fine. Go ahead."

Levine scraped the fingers of his left hand together, embarrassment reminding him of his need for a cigarette. But this was day number four, and he was going to make it. "Jack," he said, "I think maybe you ought to be the one to talk to him."

"Why me? Why not you?"

"I think he has more respect for you."

Crawley snorted. "What the hell are you talking about?"

"No, I mean it, Jack." Levine grinned self-consciously. "If I told him about it, he might think I was just dramatizing it, getting emotional or something, and he'd say thumbs down. But you're the level headed type. If you tell him it's serious, he'll believe you."

"You're nuts," said Crawley.

"You *are* the level-headed type," Levine told him. "And I *am* too emotional."

"Flattery will get you everywhere. All right, go to school."

"Thanks, Jack."

Levine shrugged into his coat and plodded out of the squadroom, downstairs, and out to the sidewalk. Lathmore Elementary was three blocks away to the right, and he walked it. There was a smell of snow in the air, but the sky was still clear. Levine strolled along sniffing the snow-tang, his hands pushed deep into the pockets of his black overcoat. The desire for a smoke was less when he was outdoors, so he didn't hurry.

Lathmore Elementary, one of the myriad private schools which have sprung up to take the place of the enfeebled public school system long since emasculated by municipal politics, was housed in an old mansion on one of the neighborhood's better blocks. The building was mainly masonry, with curved buttresses and bay windows everywhere, looming three ivy-overgrown stories to a patchwork slate roof which dipped and angled and rose crazily around to no pattern at all. Gold letters on the wide glass pane over the double-doored entrance announced the building's new function, and just inside the doors an arrow on a wall was marked "OFFICE."

Levine didn't want to have to announce himself as a policeman, but the administrative receptionist was so officious and curious that he had no choice. It was the only way he could get to see Mrs. Pidgeon, the principal, without first explaining his mission in minute detail to the receptionist.

Mrs. Pidgeon was baffled, polite, terrified and defensive, but not very much of any of them. It was as though these four emotions were being held in readiness, for one of them to spring into action as soon as she found out exactly what it was a police officer could possibly want in Lathmore Elementary. Levine tried to explain as gently and vaguely as possible:

"I'd like to talk to one of your teachers," he said. "About a little girl, a student of yours."

"What about her?"

"She made a report to us yesterday," Levine told her. "It's difficult for us to check it out, and it might help if we knew a little more about her, what her attitudes are, things like that."

Defensiveness began to edge to the fore in Mrs. Pidgeon's attitude. "What sort of report?"

"I'm sorry," said Levine. "If there's nothing to it, it would be better not to spread it."

"Something about this school?"

"Oh, no," said Levine, managing not to smile. "Not at all."

"Very well." Defensiveness receded, and a sort of cold politeness became more prominent. "You want to talk to her teacher, then."

"Yes."

"Her name?"

"Amy Walker. Amy Thornbridge Walker."

"Oh, yes!" Mrs. Pidgeon's face suddenly lit with pleasure, not at Levine but at his reminding her of that particular child. Then the pleasure gave way just as suddenly to renewed bafflement. "It's about Amy? *She* came to you yesterday?"

"That's right."

"Well." She looked helplessly around the room, aching to

find out more but unable to find a question that would get around Levine's reticence. Finally, she gave up, and asked him to wait while she went for Miss Haskell, the fifth grade teacher. Levine stood as she left the room, then sank back into the maroon leather chair, feeling bulky and awkward in this hushed heavy-draped office.

He waited five minutes before Mrs. Pidgeon returned, this time with Miss Haskell in tow. Miss Haskell, unexpectedly, was a comfortable fortyish woman in a sensible suit and flat shoes, not the thin tall bird he'd expected. He acknowledged Mrs. Pidgeon's introduction, hastily rising again, and Mrs. Pidgeon pointedly said, "Try not to be too long, Mr. Levine. You may use my office."

"Thank you."

She left, and Levine and Miss Haskell stood facing each other in the middle of the room. He motioned at a chair. "Would you sit down, please?"

"Thank you. Mrs. Pidgeon said you wanted to ask me about Amy Walker."

"Yes, I want to know what kind of child she is, anything you can tell me about her."

Miss Haskell smiled. "I can tell you she's a brilliant and well-brought-up child," she said. "That she's the one I picked to be student in charge while I came down to talk to you. That she's always at least a month ahead of the rest of the class in reading the assignments, and that she's the most practical child I've ever met."

Levine reached to his cigarette pocket, cut the motion short, awkwardly returned his hand to his side. "Her father died two weeks ago, didn't he?"

"That's right."

"How did they get along, do you know? Amy and her father."

"She worshipped him. He was her stepfather actually, having married her mother only about a year ago, I believe. Amy doesn't remember her real father. Mr. Walker was the only father she knew, and having been without one for so long——" Miss Haskell spread her hands. "He was important to her," she finished.

"She took his death hard?"

"She was out of school for a week, inconsolable. She spent the time at her grandmother's, I understand. The grandmother caters to her, of course. I believe her mother had a doctor in twice."

"Yes, her mother." Levine didn't know what to do with his hands. He clasped them in front of him. "How do Amy and her mother get along?"

"Normally, so far as I know. There's never been any sign of discord between them that I've seen." She smiled again. "But my contact with Amy is limited to school hours, of course."

"You think there is discord?"

"No, not at all. I didn't mean to imply that. Just that I couldn't give you an expert answer to the question."

Levine nodded. "You're right. Is Amy a very imaginative child?"

"She's very self-sufficient in play, if that's what you mean."

"I was thinking about story-telling."

"Oh, a liar." She shook her head. "No, Amy isn't the tall tale type. A very practical little girl, really. Very dependable judgment. As I say, she's the one I left in charge of the class."

"She wouldn't be likely to come to us with a wild story she'd made up all by herself."

"Not at all. If Amy told you about something, it's almost certainly the truth."

Levine sighed. "Thank you," he said. "Thank you very much."

Miss Haskell rose to her feet. "Could you tell me what this wild story was? I might be able to help."

"I'd rather not," he said. "Not until we're sure, one way or the other."

"If I can be of any assistance ——"

"Thank you," he said again. "You've already helped."

Back at the station, Levine entered the squadroom and hung up his coat. Crawley looked over from his desk and said, "You have all the luck, Abe. You missed the whirlwind."

"Whirlwind?"

"Amy's mama was here. Dr. Sheffield called her about you checking up on her husband's death, and just before she came over here she got a call from somebody at Lathmore Elementary, saying there was a cop there asking questions about her daughter. She didn't like us casting aspersions on her family."

"Aspersions?"

"That's what she said." Crawley grinned. "You're little Sir Echo this morning, aren't you?"

"I need a cigarette. What did the Lieutenant say?"

"She didn't talk to him. She talked to me."

"No, when you told him about the little girl's report."

"Oh. He said to take two days on it, and then let him know how it looked."

"Fine. How about Thornbridge?"

"Accidental death. Inquest said so. No question in anybody's mind. He went swimming too soon after lunch, got a stomach cramp, and drowned. What's the word on the little girl?"

"Her teacher says she's reliable. Practical and realistic. If she tells us something, it's so."

Crawley grimaced. "That isn't what I wanted to hear, Abe."

"It didn't overjoy me, either." Levine sat down at his desk. "What did the mother have to say?"

"I had to spill it, Abe. About what her daughter reported."

"That's all right," he said. "Now we've got no choice. We've got to follow though. What was her reaction?"

"She didn't believe it."

Levine shrugged. "She had to, after she thought about it."

"Sure," said Crawley. "Then she was baffled. She didn't know why Amy would say such a thing."

"Was she home when her husband died?"

"She says no." Crawley flipped open a memo pad. "Somebody had to be with him all the time, but he didn't want a professional nurse. So when Amy came home from school that afternoon, the mother went to the supermarket. Her husband was alive when she left, and dead when she got back. Or so she says."

"She says Amy was the one who found him dead?"

"No. Amy was watching television. When the mother came home, she found him, and called the doctor."

"What about noises?"

"She didn't hear any, and doesn't have any idea what Amy means."

Levine sighed. "All right," he said. "We've got one timetable discrepancy. Amy says her mother was home and made a loud noise. The mother says she was out to the supermarket." His fingers strayed to his cigarette pocket, then went on to scratch his shoulder instead. "What do you think of the mother, Jack?"

"She's tough. She was mad, and she's used to having things her own way. I can't see her playing nursemaid. But she sure seemed baffled about why the kid would make such an accusation."

"I'll have to talk to Amy again," said Levine. "Once we've got both stories, we can see which one breaks down."

Crawley said, "I wonder if she'll try to shut the kid's mouth?"

"Let's not think about that yet. We've still got all day." He reached for the phone book and looked up the number of Lathmore Elementary.

Levine talked to the girl in Mrs. Pidgeon's office at eleven o'clock. At his request, they were left alone.

Amy was dressed as neatly as she had been yesterday, and

seemed just as composed. Levine explained to her what had been done so far on the investigation, and that her mother had been told why the investigation was taking place. "I'm sorry, Amy," he said, "but we didn't have any choice. Your mother had to know."

Amy considered, solemn and formal. "I think it will be all right," she said. "She wouldn't dare try to hurt me now, with you investigating. It would be too obvious. My mother is very subtle, Mr. Levine."

Levine smiled, in spite of himself. "You have quite a vocabulary," he told her.

"I'm a very heavy reader," she explained. "Though it's difficult for me to get interesting books from the library. I'm too young, so I have to take books from the children's section." She smiled thinly. "I'll tell you a secret," she said. "I steal the ones I want to read, and then bring them back when I'm finished with them."

In a hurry, he thought, smiling, and remembered the baby next door. "I want to talk to you," he said, "about the day when your father died. Your mother said she went out to the store, and when she came back he was dead. What do you say?"

"Nonsense," she said, promptly. *"I* was the one who went out to the store. The minute I came home from school, she sent me out to the supermarket. But I came back too soon for her."

"Why?"

"Just as I was coming down the hall from the elevator, I heard a great clang sound from our apartment. Then it came again as I was opening the door. I went through the living room and saw my mother coming out of my stepfather's room. She was smiling. But then she saw me and suddenly looked terribly upset and told me something awful had happened, and she ran to the telephone to call Dr. Sheffield. She acted terribly agitated, and carried on just as though she really meant it. She fooled Dr. Sheffield completely."

"Why did you wait so long before coming to us?"

"I didn't know what to do." The solemn formality cracked all at once, and she was only a child after all, uncertain in an adult world. "I didn't think anyone would believe me, and I was afraid if Mother suspected what I knew, she might try to do something to me. But Monday in Civics Miss Haskell was talking about the duties of the different parts of government, firemen and policemen and everybody, and she said the duty of the police was to investigate crimes and see the guilty were punished. So yesterday I came and told you, because it didn't matter if you didn't believe me, you'd have to do your duty and investigate anyway."

Levine sighed. "All right," he said. "We're doing it. But we need more than just your word, you understand that, don't you? We need proof of some kind."

She nodded, serious and formal again.

"What store did you go to that day?" he asked her.

"A supermarket. The big one on Seventh Avenue."

"Do you know any of the clerks there? Would they recognize you?"

"I don't think so. It's a great big supermarket. I don't think they know any of their customers at all."

"Did you see anyone at all on your trip to the store or back, who would remember that it was you who went to the store and not your mother, and that it was that particular day?"

She considered, touching one finger to her lips as she concentrated, and finally shook her head. "I don't think so. I don't know any of the people in the neighborhood. Most of the people I know are my parents' friends or kids from school, and they live all over, not just around here."

The New York complication. In a smaller town, people know their neighbors, have some idea of the comings and goings around them. But in New York, next-door neighbors remain strangers for years. At least that was true in the apartment house sections, though less true in the quieter outlying sections like the neighborhood in which Levine lived.

Levine got to his feet. "We'll see what we can do," he said. "This clang you told me about. Do you have any idea what your mother used to make the noise?"

"No, I don't. I'm sorry. It sounded like a gong or something. I don't know what it could possibly have been."

"A tablespoon against the bottom of a pot? Something like that?"

"Oh, no. Much louder than that."

"And she didn't have anything in her hands when she came out of the bedroom?"

"No, nothing."

"Well, we'll see what we can do," he repeated. "You can go back to class now."

"Thank you," she said. "Thank you for helping me."

He smiled. "It's my duty," he said. "As you pointed out."

"You'd do it anyway, Mr. Levine," she said. "You're a very good man. Like my stepfather."

Levine touched the palm of his hand to his chest, over his heart. "Yes," he said. "In more ways than one, maybe. Well, you go back to class. Or, wait. There's one thing I can do for you."

She waited as he took a pencil and a small piece of memo paper from Mrs. Pidgeon's desk, and wrote on it the precinct phone number and his home phone number, marking which each was. "If you think there's any danger of any kind," he told her, "any trouble at all, you call me. At the precinct until four o'clock, and then at home after that."

"Thank you," she said. She folded the paper and tucked it away in the pocket of her skirt.

At a quarter to four, Levine and Crawley met again in the squadroom. When he'd come back in the morning from his talk with the little girl, Levine had found Crawley just back from having talked with Dr. Sheffield. It was Sheffield's opinion, Crawley had told him, that Amy was making the whole thing up, that her stepfather's death had been a severe shock and this was some sort of delayed reaction to it. Certainly he couldn't see any possibility that Mrs. Walker had actually murdered her husband, nor could he begin to guess at any motive for such an act.

Levine and Crawley had eaten lunch together in Wilton's, across the street from the station, and then had separated, both to try to find someone who had either seen Amy or her mother on the shopping trip the afternoon Mr. Walker had died. This, aside from the accusation of murder itself, was the only contradiction between their stories. Find proof that one was lying, and they'd have the full answer. So Levine had started at the market and Crawley at the apartment building, and they'd spent the entire afternoon up and down the neighborhood, asking their questions and getting only blank stares for answers.

Crawley was there already when Levine came slowly into the squadroom, worn from an entire afternoon on his feet, climaxed by the climb to the precinct's second floor. He looked at Crawley and shook his head. Crawley said, "Nothing? Same here. Not a damn thing."

Levine laboriously removed his overcoat and set it on the coatrack. "No one remembers," he said. "No one saw, no one knows anyone. It's a city of strangers we live in, Jack."

"It's been two weeks," said Crawley. "Their building has a doorman, but he can't remember that far back. He sees the same tenants go in and out every day, and he wouldn't be able to tell you for sure who went in or out yesterday, much less two weeks ago, he says."

Levine looked at the wall-clock. "She's home from school by now," he said.

"I wonder what they're saying to each other. If we could listen in, we'd know a hell of a lot more than we do now."

Levine shook his head. "No. Whether she's guilty or innocent, they're both saying the exact same things. The death is two weeks old. If Mrs. Walker did commit murder, she's used to the idea by now that she's gotten away with it. She'll deny everything Amy says, and try to convince the girl she's wrong. The same things in the same words as she'd use if she were innocent."

"What if she kills the kid?" Crawley asked him.

"She won't. If Amy were to disappear, or have an accident, or be killed by an intruder, we'd know the truth at once. She can't take the chance. With her husband, all she had to do was fool a doctor who was inclined to believe her in the first place. Besides, the death was a strong possibility anyway. This time, she'd be killing a healthy ten year old, and she'd be trying to fool a couple of cops who wouldn't be inclined to believe her at all." Levine grinned. "The girl is probably safer now than she was before she ever came to us," he said. "Who knows what the mother might have been planning up till now?"

"All right, that's fine so far. But what do we do now?"

"Tomorrow, I want to take a look at the Walker apartment."

"Why not right now?"

"No. Let's give her a night to get rattled. Any evidence she hasn't removed in two weeks she isn't likely to think of now." Levine shrugged. "I don't expect to find anything," he said. "I want to look at the place because I can't think of anything else to do. All we have is the unsupported word of a ten-year old child. The body can't tell us anything, because there wasn't any murder weapon. Walker died of natural causes. Proving they were induced won't be the easiest job in the world."

"If only *somebody,*" said Crawley angrily, "had seen that kid at the grocery store! That's the only chink in the wall, Abe, the only damn place we can get a grip."

"We can try again tomorrow," said Levine, "but I doubt we'll get anywhere." He looked up as the door opened, and Trent and Kasper came in, two of the men on the four to midnight shift. "Tomorrow," he repeated. "Maybe lightning will strike."

"Maybe," said Crawley.

Levine shrugged back into his overcoat and left the office for the day. When he got home, he broke his normal habit and went straight into the house, not staying on the porch to read his paper. He went out to the kitchen and sat there, drinking coffee, while he filled Peg in on what little progress they'd made on the case during the day. She asked questions, and he answered them, offered suggestions and he mulled them over and rejected them, and throughout the evening, every once in a while, one or the other of them would find some other comment to make, but neither of them got anywhere. The girl seemed to be reasonably safe, at least for a while, but that was the best that could be said.

The baby next door was crying when they went to bed together at eleven o'clock. The baby kept him awake for a while, and his thoughts on the Walker death revolved and revolved, going nowhere. Once or twice during the evening, he had absent-mindedly reached for a cigarette, but had barely noticed the motion. His concentration and concern for Amy Walker and her mother was strong enough now to make him forget his earlier preoccupation with the problem of giving up smoking. Now, lying awake in the dark, the thought of cigarettes didn't even enter his head. He went over and over what the mother had said, what the daughter had told him, and gradually he drifted off into deep, sound sleep.

He awoke in a cold sweat, suddenly knowing the truth. It was as though he'd dreamed it, or someone had whispered it in his ear, and now he knew for sure.

She would kill tonight, and she would get away with it. He knew how she'd do it, and when, and there'd be no way to get her for it, no proof, nothing, no way at all.

He sat up, trembling, cold in the dark room, and reached

out to the nightstand for his cigarettes. He pawed around on the nightstand, and suddenly remembered, and pounded the nightstand with his fist in frustration and rage. She'd get away with it!

If he could get there in time— He could stop her, if he got there in time. He pushed the covers out of the way and climbed from the bed. Peg murmured in her sleep and burrowed deeper into the pillow. He gathered his clothes and crept from the bedroom.

He turned the light on in the living room. The clock over the television set read ten till one. There might still be time, she might be waiting until she was completely asleep. Unless she was going to do it with pills, something to help sleep, to make sleep a permanent, everlasting sure thing.

He grabbed the phone book and looked up the number of one of the private cab companies on Avenue L. He dialed, and told the dispatcher it was urgent, and the dispatcher said a car would be there in five minutes.

He dressed hurriedly, in the living room, then went out to the kitchen for pencil and paper, and left Peg a short note. "I had to go out for a while. Be back soon." In case she woke up. He left it on the nightstand.

A horn sounded briefly out front and he hurried to the front of the house, turning off lights. As he went trotting down the walk toward the cab, the baby next door cried out. He registered the sound, thought, *Baby next door,* and dismissed it from his mind. He had no time for extraneous thoughts, about babies or cigarettes or the rasp of his breathing from only this little exertion, running from the house. He gave the address, Prospect Park West, and sat back in the seat as the cab took off. It was a strange feeling, riding in a cab. He couldn't remember the last time he'd done it. It was a luxuriant feeling. To go so fast with such relaxing calm. If only it was fast enough.

It cost him four dollars, including the tip. If she was still alive, it was the bargain of the century. But as he hurried into the building and down the long narrow lobby to the elevators, the sound he'd heard as he'd left his home came back to him, he heard it again in his memory, and all at once he realized it hadn't been the baby next door at all. It had been the telephone.

He pressed the elevator button desperately, and the elevator slid slowly down to him from the eleventh floor. It had been the ring of the telephone.

So she'd made her move already. He was too late. When he'd left the house, he'd been too late.

The elevator doors opened, and he stepped in, pushed the button marked 4. He rode upward.

He could visualize that phone call. The little girl, hushed, terrified, whispering, beseeching. And Peg, half-awake, reading his note to her. And he was too late.

The door to apartment 4-A was ajar, the interior dark. He reached to his hip, but he'd been in too much of a hurry. The gun was at home, on the dresser.

He stepped across the threshold, cautiously, peering into the dark. Dim light spilled in from the hallway, showing him only this section of carpet near the door. The rest of the apartment was pitch black.

He felt the wall beside the door, found the light switch and clicked it on.

The light in the hall went out.

He tensed, the darkness now complete. A penny in the socket? And this was an old building, in which the tenants didn't pay directly for their own electricity, so the hall light was on the same line as the foyer of apartment A on every floor. They must have blown a fuse once, and she'd noticed that.

But why? What was she trying for?

The telephone call, as he was leaving the house. Somehow or other, she'd worked it out, and she knew that Levine was on his way here, that Levine knew the truth.

He backed away toward the doorway. He needed to get to

the elevator, to get down and away from here. He'd call the precinct. They'd need flashlights, and numbers. This darkness was no place for him, alone.

A face rose toward him, luminous, staring, grotesque, limned in pale cold green, a staring devil face shining in green fire against the blackness. He cried out, instinctive panic filling his mouth with bile, and stumbled backwards away from the thing, bumping painfully into the doorpost. And the face disappeared.

He felt around him, his hands shaking, all sense of direction lost. He had to get out, he had to find the door. She was trying to kill him, she knew he knew and she was trying to kill him the same way she'd killed Walker. Trying to stop his heart.

A shriek jolted into his ears, loud, loud, incredibly loud, magnified far beyond the power of the human voice, a world-filling scream of hatred, grating him to the bone, and his flailing hands touched a wall, he leaned against it trembling. His mouth was open, straining for air, his chest was clogged, his heart beat fitfully, like the random motions of a wounded animal. The echoes of the shriek faded away, and then it sounded again, even louder, all around him, vibrating him like a fly on a pin.

He pushed away from the wall, blind and panic-stricken, wanting only to get away, to be away, out of this horror, and he stumbled into an armchair, lost his balance, fell heavily forward over the chair and rolled to the floor.

He lay there, gasping, unthinking, as brainlessly terrified as a rabbit in a trapper's snare. Pinwheels of light circled the corners of his stinging eyes, every straining breath was a searing fire in his throat. He lay on his back, encumbered and helpless in the heavy overcoat, arms and legs curled upward in feeble defense, and waited for the final blow.

But it didn't come. The silence lengthened, the blackness of the apartment remained unbroken, and gradually rationality came back to him and he could close his mouth, painfully swallow saliva, lower his arms and legs, and listen.

Nothing. No sound.

She'd heard him fall, that was it. And now she was waiting, to be sure he was dead. If she heard him move again, she'd hurl another thunderbolt, but for now she was simply waiting.

And the wait gave him his only chance. The face had been only phosphorescent paint on a balloon, pricked with a pin when he cried out. The shriek had come, most likely, from a tape recorder. Nothing that could kill him, nothing that could injure him, if only he kept in his mind what they were, and what she was trying to do.

My heart is weak, he thought, *but not that weak. Not as weak as Walker's, still recovering from his first attack. It could kill Walker, but it couldn't quite kill me:*

He lay there, recuperating, calming, coming back to himself. And then the flashlight flicked on, and the beam was aimed full upon him.

He raised his head, looked into the light. He could see nothing behind it. "No, Amy," he said. "It didn't work."

The light flicked off.

"Don't waste your time," he said into the darkness. "If it didn't work at first, when I wasn't ready for it, it won't work at all.

"Your mother is dead," he said, speaking softly, knowing she was listening, that so long as she listened she wouldn't move. He raised himself slowly to a sitting position. "You killed her, too. Your father and mother both. And when you called my home, to tell me that she'd killed herself, and my wife told you I'd already left, you knew then that I knew. And you had to kill me, too. I'd told you that my heart was weak, like your father's. So you'd kill me, and it would simply be another heart failure, brought on by the sight of your mother's corpse."

The silence was deep and complete, like a forest pool.

Levine shifted, gaining his knees, moving cautiously and without sound.

"Do you want to know how I knew?" he asked her. "Monday in Civics Miss Haskell told you about the duties of the police. But Miss Haskell told me that you were always at least a month ahead in your studies. Two weeks before your stepfather died, you read that assignment in your schoolbook, and then and there you decided how to kill them both."

He reached out his hand, cautiously, touched the chair he'd tripped over, shifted his weight that way, and came slowly to his feet, still talking. "The only thing I don't understand," he said, "is why. You steal books from the library that they won't let you read. Was this the same thing to you? Is it all it was?"

From across the room, she spoke, for the first time. "You'll never understand, Mr. Levine," she said. That young voice, so cold and adult and emotionless, speaking out contemptuously to him in the dark.

And all at once he could *see* the way it had been with Walker. Somnolent in the bed, listening to the frail fluttering of the weary heart, as Levine often lay at night, listening and wondering. And suddenly that shriek, out of the midafternoon stillness, coming from nowhere and everywhere, driving in at him —

Levine shivered. "No," he said. "It's you who don't understand. To steal a book, to snuff out a life, to you they're both the same. You don't understand at all."

She spoke again, the same cold contempt still in her voice. "It was bad enough when it was only *her*. Don't do this, don't do that. But then she had to marry him, and there were two of them watching me all the time, saying no no no, that's all they ever said. The only time I could ever have some peace was when I was at my grandmother's."

"Is *that* why?" He could hear again the baby crying, the gigantic ego of the very young, the imperious demand that *they* be attended to. And in the place of terror, he now felt only rage. That this useless half-begun thing should kill, and kill —

"Do you know what's going to happen to you?" he asked her. "They won't execute you, you're too young. They'll judge you insane, and they'll lock you away. And there'll be guards and matrons there, to say don't do this and don't do that, a million million times more than you can imagine. And they'll keep you locked away in a little room, forever and ever, and they'll let you do *nothing* you want to do, *nothing.*"

He moved now, feeling his way around the chair, reaching out to touch the wall, working his way carefully toward the door. "There's nothing you can do to me now," he said. "Your bag of tricks won't work, and I won't drink the poison you fed your mother. And no one will believe the suicide confession you forged. I'm going to phone the precinct, and they'll come and get you, and you'll be locked away in that tiny room, forever and ever."

The flashlight hit the floor with a muffled thud, and then he heard her running, away from him, deeper into the apartment. He crossed the room with cautious haste, hands out before him, and felt around on the floor till his fingers blundered into the flashlight. He picked it up, clicked it on, and followed.

He found her in her mother's bedroom, standing on the window sill. The window was wide open, and the December wind keened into the room. The dead woman lay reposed on the bed, the suicide note conspicuous on the nightstand. He shone the light full on the girl, and she warned him, "Stay away. Stay away from me."

He walked toward her. "They'll lock you away," he said. "In a tiny, tiny room."

"No, they won't!" And she was gone from the window.

Levine breathed, knowing what he had done, that he had made it end this way. She hadn't ever understood death, and so it was possible for her to throw herself into it. The parents begin the child, and the child ends the parents. A white rage flamed in him at the thought.

He stepped to the window and looked down at the broken doll on the sidewalk far below. In another apartment, above his head, a baby wailed, creasing the night. *Make way, make way.*

He looked up. "We will," he whispered. "We will. But in our own time. Don't rush us."

THE DEATH OF A BUM

Abraham Levine of Brooklyn's Forty-Third Precinct sat at his desk in the squadroom and wished Jack Crawley would get well soon. Crawley, his usual tour partner, was in the hospital recovering from a bullet in the leg, and Levine was working now with a youngster recently assigned to the squad, a college graduate named Andy Stettin. Levine liked the boy — though he sometimes had the feeling Stettin was picking his brains — but there was an awkwardness in the work without Crawley.

He was sitting now at the desk, thinking about Jack Crawley, when the telephone rang. He answered, saying, "Forty-Third Precinct. Levine."

It was a woman's voice, middle-aged, very excited. "There's a man been murdered! You've got to come right away!"

Levine pulled pencil and paper close, then said, "Your name, please?"

"There's been a murder! Don't you understand ── "

"Yes, ma'am. May I have your name, please?"

"Mrs. Francis Temple. He's lying right upstairs."

"The address, please?"

"One ninety-eight Third Street. I told all this to the other man, I don't see ── "

"And you say there's a dead man there?"

"He's been shot! I just went in to change the linen, and he was lying there!"

"Someone will be there right away." He hung up as she was starting another sentence, and looked up to see Stettin, a tall athletic young man with dark-rimmed glasses and a blond crewcut, standing by the door, already wearing his coat.

"Just a second," Levine said, and dialed for Mulvane, on the desk downstairs. "This is Abe. Did you just transfer a call from Mrs. Francis Temple to my office?"

"I did. The beat car's on the way."

"All right. Andy and I are taking it."

Levine cradled the phone and got to his feet. He went over and took his coat from the rack and shrugged into it, then followed the impatient Stettin downstairs to the car.

That was another thing. Crawley had always driven the Chevy. But Stettin drove too fast, was too quick to hit the siren and gun through busy intersections, so now Levine had to do the driving, a chore he didn't enjoy.

The address was on a block of ornate nineteenth-century brownstones, now all converted either into furnished apartments or boarding houses. One ninety-eight was furnished apartments, and Mrs. Francis Temple was its landlady. She was waiting on the top step of the stoop, wringing her hands, a buxom fiftyish woman in a black dress and open black sweater, a maroon knit shawl over her head to keep out the cold.

The prowl car was double-parked in front of the house, and Levine braked the Chevy to a stop behind it. He and

Stettin climbed out, crossed the sidewalk, and went up the stoop.

Mrs. Temple was on the verge of panic. Her hands kept washing each other, she kept shifting her weight back and forth from one foot to the other, and she stared bug-eyed as the detectives came up the stoop toward her.

"Are you police?" she demanded, her voice shrill.

Levine dragged out his wallet, showed her the badge. "Are the patrolmen up there?" he asked.

She nodded, stepping aside to let him move past her. "I went in to change the linen, and there he was, lying in the bed, all covered with blood. It was terrible, terrible."

Levine went on in, Stettin after him, and Mrs. Temple brought up the rear, still talking. Levine interrupted her to ask, "Which room?"

"The third floor front," she said, and went back to repeating how terrible it had been when she'd gone in there and seen him on the bed, covered with blood.

Stettin was too eager for conscious politeness. He bounded on up the maroon-carpeted stairs, while Levine plodded up after him, the woman one step behind all the way, the shawl still over her head.

One of the patrolmen was standing in the open doorway at the other end of the third-floor hall. As was usual in this type of brownstone, the upper floors consisted of two large rooms rented separately, each with a small kitchenette but both sharing the same bath. The dead man was in the front room.

Levine said to the woman, "Wait out here, please," nodded to the patrolman, and went on through into the room.

Stettin and the second patrolman were over to the right, by the studio couch, talking together. Their forms obscured Levine's view of the couch as he came through the doorway, and he got the feeling, as he had had more than once with the energetic Stettin, that he was Stettin's assistant rather than the other way around.

Which was ridiculous, of course. Stettin turned, clearing Levine's view, saying, "How's it look to you, Abe?"

The studio couch had been opened up and was now in its other guise, that of a linen-covered bed. Between the sheets the corpse lay peaceably on its back with the covers tucked up around the sheets and rested stiffly on its chest.

Levine came over and stood by the bed, looking down at it. The bullet had struck the bridge of the nose, smashing bone and cartilage, and discoloring the flesh around it. There was hardly any nose left. The mouth hung open, and the top front teeth had been jarred partially out of their sockets by the force of the bullet.

The slain man had bled profusely, and the pillow and the turned-down sheet around his throat were drenched with blood.

The top blanket was blue, and was now scattered with smallish chunks of white stuff. Levine reached down and picked up one of the white chunks, feeling it between his fingers.

"Potato," he said, more to himself than to the cop at his side.

Stettin said, "What's that?"

"Potato. That stuff on the bed. He used a potato for a silencer."

Stettin smiled blankly. "I don't follow you, Abe."

Levine moved his hands in demonstration as he described what he meant. "The killer took a raw potato, and jammed the barrel of the gun into it. Then, when he fired, the bullet smashed through the potato, muffling the sound. It's a kind of home-made silencer."

Stettin nodded, and glanced again at the body. "Think it was a gang killing, then?"

"I don't know," Levine replied, frowning. He turned to the patrolman. "What have you got?"

The patrolman dragged a flat black notebook out of his hip pocket, and flipped it open. "He's the guy that rented the place. The landlady identified him. He gave his name as Maurice Gold."

Excited, Stettin said, "Morry Gold?" He came closer to the bed, squinting down at the face remnant as though he could see it better that way. "Yeah, by God, it is," he said, his expression grim. "It *was* a gang killing, Abe!"

"You know him?"

"I saw him once. On the lineup downtown, maybe — two months ago."

Levine smiled thinly. Leave it to Stettin, he thought. Most detectives considered the lineup a chore and a waste of time, and grumbled every time their turn came around to go downtown and attend. The line-up was supposed to familiarize the precinct detectives with the faces of known felons, but it took a go-getter like Stettin to make the theory work. Levine had been attending the lineup twice a month for fifteen years and hadn't once recognized one of the felons later on.

Stettin was turning his head this way and that, squinting at the body again. "Yeah, sure," he said. "Morry Gold. He had a funny way of talking — a Cockney accent, maybe. That's him, all right."

"What was he brought in for?"

"Possession of stolen goods. He was a fence. I remember the Chief talking to him. I guess he'd been brought in lots of times before." He shook his head. "Apparently he managed to wriggle out of it."

The patrolman said, "He'd have been much better off if he hadn't."

"A falling out among thieves," said Stettin. "Think so, Abe?"

"It could be." To the patrolman, he said, "Anything else?"

"He lived here not quite two years. That's what the landlady told me. She found him at quarter after four, and the last time she saw him alive was yesterday, around seven o'clock in the evening. He went out then. He must have come back some time after eleven o'clock, when the landlady went to bed. Otherwise, she'd have seen him come in." He grinned without humor. "She's one of those," he said.

"I'll go talk to her." Levine looked over at the body again, and averted his eyes. An old English epitaph flickered through his mind: *As you are, so was I; as I am, so you will be.* Twenty-four years as a cop hadn't hardened him to the tragic and depressing finality of death, and in the last few years, as he had moved steadily into the heart-attack range and as the inevitability of his own end had become more and more real to him, he had grown steadily more vulnerable to the dread implicit in the sight of death.

He turned away, saying, "Andy, give the place a going-over. Address book, phone numbers, somebody's name in the flyleaf of a book. You know the kind of thing."

"Sure." Stettin glanced around, eager to get at it. "Do you think he'd have any of the swag here?"

The word sounded strange on Stettin's tongue, odd and archaic. Levine smiled, as the death-dread wore off, and said, "I doubt it. Stick around here for the M.E. and the technical crew. Get the time of death and whatever else they can give you."

"Sure thing."

Mrs. Francis Temple was still outside in the hall, jabbering now at the second patrolman, who was making no attempt to hide his boredom. Levine took her away, much to the patrolman's relief, and they went downstairs to her cellar apartment, the living room of which was Gay Nineties from end to end, from the fringed beaded lampshades to the marble porcelain vases on the mantle.

In these surroundings, Mrs. Temple's wordiness switched from the terrible details of her discovery of the body to the nostalgic details of her life with her late husband, who had been a newspaperman.

Levine, by main force, wrestled the conversation back to

the present, in order to ask his questions about Maurice Gold. "What did he do for a living," he asked. "Do you know?"

"He said he was a salesman. Sometimes he was gone nearly a week at a time."

"Do you know what he sold?"

She shook her head. "There were never any samples or anything in his room," she said. "I would have noticed them." She shivered suddenly, hugging herself, and said, "What a terrible thing. You don't know what it was like, to come into the room and see him ——"

Levine thought he knew. He thought he knew better than Mrs. Temple. He said, "Did he have many visitors? Close friends, that you know about?"

"Well —— There were two or three men who came by sometimes in the evenings. I believe they played cards."

"Do you know their names?"

"No, I'm sorry. I really didn't know Mr. Gold very well — not as a friend. He was a very close-mouthed man." One hand fluttered to her lips. "Oh, listen to me. The poor man is lying dead, and listen to me talking about him."

"Did anyone else ever come by?" Levine persisted. "Besides these three men he played cards with."

She shook her head. "Not that I remember. I think he was a lonely man. Lonely people can recognize one another, and I've been lonely, too, since Alfred died. These last few years have been difficult for me, Mr. Levine."

It took Levine ten minutes to break away from the woman gently, without learning anything more. "We'd like to try to identify his card-playing friends," he said. "Would you have time to come look at pictures this afternoon?"

"Well, yes, of course. It was a terrible thing, Mr. Levine, an absolutely terrible ——"

"Yes, ma'am."

Levine escaped, to find Stettin coming back downstairs, loose-limbed and athletic. Feeling a little bit guilty at palming the voluble Mrs. Temple off on his partner, Levine said, "Take Mrs. Temple to look at some mug shots, will you? Known former acquaintances of Gold—or anyone she recognizes. She says there were two or three men who used to come here to play cards."

"Will do." Stettin paused at the foot of the steps. "Uh, Abe," he said, "we don't have to break our humps over this one, do we?"

"What do you mean?"

"Well——" Stettin shrugged, and nodded his head at the stairs. "He was just a bum, you know. A small-time crook. The world's better off without him."

"He was alive," said Levine. "And now he's dead."

"Okay, okay. For Pete's sake, I wasn't saying we should forget the whole thing—just that we shouldn't break our humps over it."

"We'll do our job," Levine told him, "just as though he'd had the keys to the city and money in fifty-seven banks."

"Okay. You didn't have to get sore, Abe."

"I'm not sore. Take Mrs. Temple in the car. I'm going to stay here a while and ask some more questions. Mrs. Temple's in her apartment there."

"Okay."

"Oh, by the way. When you get out to the car, call in and have somebody get us the dope on that arrest two months ago. Find out if you can whether there was anybody else involved, and if by chance the arresting officer knows any of Gold's friends. Anything like that."

"Will do."

Levine went on upstairs to ask questions.

The other tenants knew even less than Mrs. Temple. Levine was interrupted for a while by a reporter, and by the time he'd finished questioning the tenants it was past four o'clock, and late enough for him to go off duty. He phoned the precinct, and then went on home.

The following morning he arrived at the precinct at eight o'clock for his third and last day-shift on this cycle. Stettin was already there, sitting at Levine's desk and looking through a folder. He leaped to his feet, grinning and ebullient as ever, saying, "Hiya, Abe. We got us some names."

"Good."

Levine eased himself into his chair, and Stettin hovered over him, opening the folder. "The arresting officer was a Patrolman Michaels, out of the Thirtieth. I couldn't find out why the charge didn't stick, because Michaels was kind of touchy about that. I guess he made some kind of procedural goof. But anyhow, he gave me some names. Gold has a brother, Abner, who runs a pawnshop in East New York. Michaels says Gold was a kind of go-between for his brother. Morry would buy the stolen goods, cache it, and then transfer it to Abner's store."

Levine nodded. "Anything else?"

"Well, Gold took one fall, about nine years ago. He was caught accepting a crate full of stolen furs. The thief was caught with him." Stettin pointed to a name and address. "That's him — Elly Kapp. Kapp got out last year, and that's his last known address."

"You've been doing good work," Levine told him. He grinned up at Stettin and said, "Been breaking your hump?"

Stettin grinned back, in embarrassment. "I can't help it," he said. "You know me, old Stettin Fetchit."

Levine nodded. He'd heard Stettin use the line before. It was his half-joking apology for being a boy on the way up, surrounded by stodgy plodders like Abe Levine.

"Okay," said Levine. "Anything from Mrs. Temple?"

"One positive identification, and a dozen maybes. The positive is a guy named Sal Casetta. He's a small-time bookie."

Levine got to his feet. "Let's go talk to these three," he said. "The brother first."

Twenty-two minutes later they were in the East New York pawnshop. Abner Gold was a stocky man with thinning hair and thick spectacles. He was also—once Levine had flashed the police identification—very nervous.

"Come into the office," he said. "Please, please. Come into the office."

Levine noticed that the thick accent Gold had worn when they'd first come in had suddenly vanished.

Gold unlocked the door to the cage, relocked it after them, and led the way back past the bins to his office, a small and crowded room full of ledgers. There was a rolltop desk, a metal filing cabinet and four sagging leather chairs.

"Sit down, sit down," he said. "You've come about my brother."

"You've been notified?"

"I read about it in the *News*. A terrible way to hear, believe me."

"I'm sure it must be," Levine said.

He hesitated. Usually, Jack Crawley handled the questioning, while Levine observed silently from a corner. But Jack was still laid up with the bad leg, and Levine wasn't sure Stettin—eager though he might be—would know the right questions or how to ask them. So it was up to him.

Levine sighed, and said, "When was the last time you saw your brother, Mr. Gold?"

Gold held his hands out to the sides, in a noncommittal shrug. "A week ago? Two weeks?"

"You're not sure."

"I think two weeks. You must understand, my brother and I—we'd drifted apart."

"Because of his trouble with the law?"

Gold nodded. "A part of it, yes. God rest his soul, Mister——?"

"Levine."

"Yes. God rest his soul, Mister Levine, but I must tell you what's in my heart. You have to know the truth. Maurice

130

was not a good man. Do you understand me? He was my brother, and now he's been murdered, but still I must say it. His life went badly for him, Mr. Levine, and he became sour. When he was young—" He shrugged again. "He became very bitter, I think. He lost his belief."

"His faith, you mean?"

"Oh, that, too. Maurice was not a religious man. But even more than that, do you follow me? He lost his *belief*. In the goodness of man—in *life*. Do you understand me?"

"I think so." Levine watched Gold's face carefully. Stettin had said that the brothers had worked together in the buying and selling of stolen goods, but Abner Gold was trying very hard to convince them of his own innocence. Levine wasn't sure yet whether or not he could be convinced.

"The last time you saw him," he said, "did he act nervous at all? As though he was expecting trouble?"

"Maurice always expected trouble. But I do know what you mean. No, nothing like that, nothing more than his usual pessimism."

"Do you yourself know of any enemies he might have made?"

"Ever since I read the article in the paper, I've been asking myself exactly that question. Did anyone hate my brother enough to want to kill him. But I can think of no one. You must understand me, I didn't know my brother's associates. We—drifted apart."

"You didn't know any of his friends at all?"

"I don't believe so, no."

"Not Sal Casetta?"

"An Italian? No, I don't know him." Gold glanced at Stettin, then leaned forward to say to Levine, "Excuse me, do you mind? Could I speak to you alone for a moment?"

"Sure," said Stettin promptly. "I'll wait outside."

"Thank you. Thank you very much." Gold beamed at Stettin until he left, then leaned toward Levine again. "I can talk to you," he said. "Not in front of the other policeman."

Levine frowned, but said nothing.

"Listen to me," said Gold. His eyes were dark, and deepest. "Maurice was my brother. If anyone has the right to say what I am going to say now it is me, the brother. Maurice is better dead. Better for everyone. The police are shorthanded, I know this. You have so much work; forget Maurice. No one wants vengeance. Listen to me, I am his brother. Who has a better right to talk?"

You're talking to the wrong man, Levine thought. *Stettin's the one who thinks your way.* But he kept quiet, and waited.

Gold paused, his hands out as though in offering, presenting his ideas to Levine. Then he lowered his hands and leaned back and said, "You understand me. That's why I wanted to talk to you alone. You are a policeman, sworn to uphold the law, this new law in this new country. But I am speaking to you now from the old law. You follow me, Levine. And if I say to you, I don't want vengeance for the slaying of my brother, I speak within a law that is older and deeper."

"A law that says murder should be ignored and forgotten? A law that says life doesn't matter? I never heard of it."

"Levine, you know what law I'm talking about! I'm his brother, and I —— "

"You're a fool, Gold, and that's the damnedest bribe I've ever been offered."

"Bribe?" Gold seemed shocked at the thought. "I didn't offer you any —— "

"What do I do to belong, Gold? I send in the label from a package of Passover candles, and then what do I get? I learn all about the secret handshake, and I get the ring with the secret compartment, and I get the magic decodifier so we can send each other messages others won't understand. Is that it?"

"You shouldn't mock what —— "

"Is there anything you wouldn't use, Gold? Do you have respect for anything at all?"

Gold looked away, his expression stony. "I thought I could talk to you," he said. "I thought you would understand."

"I do understand," Levine told him. "Get on your feet."

"What?"

"You're coming back to the precinct to answer some more questions."

"But — but I've *told* you — " Gold started to say.

"You told me you didn't want your brother's murderer found. After a while, you'll tell me why. On your feet."

"For God's sake, Levine — "

"Get on your feet!"

It was a small room. The echoes of his shout came back to his ears, and he suddenly realized he'd lost his temper despite himself, and his left hand jerked automatically to his chest, pressing there to feel for the heartbeat. He had a skip, every eighth beat or so, and when he allowed himself to get excited the skipping came closer together. That irregularity of rhythm was the most pronounced symptom he had to support his fear of heart trouble and it was never very far from his consciousness. He pressed his hand to his chest now, feeling the thumping within, and the skip, and counted from there to the next skip . . . seven.

He took a deep breath. Quietly he said, "Come along, Gold. Don't make me call in the other policeman to carry you."

Abraham Levine couldn't bring himself to grill Gold personally after all; he was afraid he'd lose control. So he simply filled Stettin in on what had been said, and what he wanted to know. Stettin took care of the questioning, with assists from Andrews and Campbell, two of the other detectives now on duty, while Levine left the precinct again, to find Sal Casetta.

Casetta lived in the New Utrecht section of Brooklyn, in a brick tenement on 79th Street. It was a walk-up, and the bookmaker's apartment was on the fourth floor. Levine climbed the stairs slowly, stopping to rest at each landing. When he got to the fourth floor, he paused to catch his breath, and light a cigarette before knocking on the door marked 14.

A woman answered—a short blowsy woman in a loose sweater and a tight black skirt. She was barefooted, and her feet were dirty, her toenails enameled a deep red. She looked challengingly at Levine.

Levine said, "I'm looking for Sal Casetta."

"He ain't home."

"Where can I find him?"

"What do you want him for?"

"Police," said Levine. "I don't want to talk to him about bookmaking. A friend of his was killed; maybe he could help us."

"What makes you think he wants to help you?"

"It was a friend of his that was killed."

"So what? You ain't a friend of his."

"If Sal was killed," Levine said, "and I was looking for his murderer, would you help me?"

The woman grimaced, and shrugged uneasily. "I told you he wasn't here," she said.

"Just tell me where I can find him."

She thought it over. She was chewing gum, and her jaw moved continuously for a full minute. Finally, she shrugged again and said, "Come on in. I'll go get him for you."

"Thank you."

She led the way into a small living room, with soiled drapes at the windows, and not enough furniture. "Grab a seat any place," she said. "Look out for roaches."

Levine thanked her again, and sat down gingerly on an unpainted wooden chair.

"What was the name of the friend?" she asked.

"Morry Gold."

"Oh, *that* bum." Her mouth twisted around its wad of gum. "Why waste time on him?"

"Because he was killed," said Levine.

"You want to make work for yourself," she told him, "it's no skin off my nose. Wait here, I'll be right back."

While he waited Levine's thoughts kept reverting to Morry Gold. After about ten minutes, he heard the front door open, and a few seconds later the woman came back accompanied by a short, heavyset man with bushy black hair and rather shifty eyes.

He came in nodding his head jerkily, saying, "I read about it in the papers. I read about it this morning."

"You're Sal Casetta?"

"Yeah, yeah, that's right, that's me. You're a cop, huh?"

Levine showed his badge, then said, "You used to play cards with Morry Gold?"

"Yeah, sure, that's right. Poker. Quarter, half-dollar. Friendly game, you know."

"Who were the other players?" Levine asked.

"Well, uh——" Casetta glanced nervously at the woman, and rubbed the back of his hand across his nose. "Well, you know how it is. You don't feel right about giving out names."

"Why? Do you think one of them killed Gold?"

"Hey now—Listen. We're all friends. Nothing like that. *I* wouldn't want to bump Morry, and neither would those guys. We're all buddies."

"Then give me their names."

Casetta cleared his throat, and glanced at the woman again, and scuffed his feet on the floor. Finally, he said, "Well, all right. But don't tell them you got it from me, huh?"

"Gold's landlady identified you," Levine told him. "She could have identified the other two."

"Yeah, sure, that's right. So it's Jake Mosca—that's like Moscow, only with an 'a'—and Barney Feldman. Okay?"

Levine copied the names down. "You know where they live?"

"Naw, not me."

"We'll leave that a blank, then. When was the last game?"

"At Morry's? That was on Saturday. Right, baby?"

The woman nodded. "Saturday," she said.

"Did Gold act nervous or depressed Saturday?"

"You mean, did he know he was gonna get it? Not a bit. Calm like always, you know?"

"Do you have any idea who might have wanted to kill him?"

"Not me. I know Morry from when we used to live in the same neighborhood, that's all. His business is his business."

"You wouldn't know who his enemies were."

"That's right. If Morry had enemies, he never said nothing to me."

"What about other friends?"

"Friends?" Casetta rubbed his nose again, then said, "We didn't see each other that much since we moved away. Just for the games. Uh, wait a second. There was another guy came in the game for a while, Arnie something. A fish, a real fish. So after a while he quit."

"You don't remember his last name?"

Casetta shook his head. "Just Arnie something. Maybe Jake or Barney knows."

"All right. Do you know Gold's brother, Abner?"

"Naw, I never met him. Morry talked about him sometimes. They didn't get along."

Levine got to his feet. "Thank you very much," he said.

"Yeah, sure. Morry was okay."

"Oh, one thing more. What about women? Did he have any woman friends that you know about?"

"I never seen him with a woman," Casetta said.

"Saturday at the game, did he seem to have an unusual amount of money on him? Or did he seem very broke? How did he seem to be fixed?"

"Like always. Nothing special, pretty well heeled but nothing spectacular, you know?" Casetta looked around, at the woman, at the apartment. "Like me," he said.

Elly Kapp's last known address was in Gravesend, off Avenue X, and since Kapp had once been caught turning stolen goods over to Morry Gold it occurred to Levine that the man might know whom Gold had been dealing with lately. He might even be still selling to Gold himself.

There was no Kapp listed among the mailboxes at the address. Levine pressed the bell-button beneath the metal plate reading *Superintendent,* and several minutes later a slow-rolling fat woman with receding gray hair appeared in the doorway, holding the door open a scant three inches. She said nothing, only stared mistrustfully, so Levine dragged out his wallet and showed his identification.

"I'm looking for Elly Kapp," he said.

"Don't live here no more."

"Where does he live now?"

"I don't know." She started to close the door, but Levine held it open with the palm of his hand. "When did he move?" he demanded.

The woman shrugged. "Who remembers?" Her eyes were dull, and watched his mouth rather than his eyes. "Who cares where he went, or what he's done?"

Levine moved his hand away, and allowed the woman to close the door. He watched through the glass as she turned and rolled slowly back across the inner vestibule. Her ankles were swollen like sausages. When she disappeared in the gloom just beyond Levine turned away and went back down the stoop to the Chevy.

He drove slowly back to the precinct. Indifference breathed in the air all around him, sullen and surly. *No man is important,* the streets seemed to be saying. *Man is only useful as long as he breathes. Once the breathing stops, he is forgotten. Time stretches away beyond him, smooth and slick and with no handholds. The man is dead, and almost as swiftly as a dropped heartbeat, the space which he occupied yawns emptily and there is nothing left of him but a name.*

At times, another man is paid to remember the name long enough to carve it on stone, and the stone is set in the earth, and immediately it begins to sink. But the man is gone long since. What does it matter if he stopped a second ago or a century ago or a millenium ago? He stopped, he is no more, he is forgotten. Who cares?

Levine saw the red light just in time, and jammed on the brakes. He sat hunched over the wheel, unnerved at having almost run the light, and strove to calm himself. His breathing was labored, as though he'd been running, and he knew that the beating of his heart was erratic and heavy. He inhaled, very slowly, and let his breath out even more slowly while he waited for the light to change.

The instant it became green he drove on across the intersection. He was calmer now. The death of Morry Gold had affected him too much, and he told himself he had to snap out of it. He knew, after all, the reason he was so affected. It was because Morry Gold's death had been greeted by such universal indifference.

Almost always, the victim of a homicide is survived by relatives and friends who are passionately concerned with his end, and make a nuisance of themselves by badgering the police for quick results. With such rallying, the dead man doesn't seem quite so forlorn, quite so totally alone and forgotten.

In the interrogation room down the hall from the squad-room, Stettin and Andrews and Campbell were questioning Abner Gold. Levine stuck his head in, nodded at Stettin, avoided looking at Gold, and immediately shut the door again. He turned away and walked slowly back down the hall toward the squadroom. He heard the door behind him open and close, and then Stettin, in long easy strides, had come up even with him.

Stettin shook his head. "Nothing, Abe," he said.

"No explanation?"

"Not from him. He won't say a word any more. Not until he calls a lawyer."

Levine shook his head tiredly. He knew the type. Abner Gold's one lone virtue would be patience. He would sit in silence, and wait, and wait until eventually the detectives found his stubborn silence intolerable, and then he knew he would be allowed to go home.

"I have an explanation," Stettin said. "He's afraid of an investigation. He's afraid if we dig too deep we'll come up with proof he, worked with his brother."

"Maybe," said Levine. "Or maybe he's afraid we'll come up with proof he killed his brother."

"What for?"

"I don't know. For cheating him on some kind of deal. For blackmailing him. Your guess is as good as mine."

Stettin shrugged. "We can keep asking," he said. "But he can keep right on not answering until we can no longer stand the sight of him."

Levine glanced at his watch. Quarter to one. He'd stopped off for lunch on the way back. He said, "I'll go talk to him for a while."

"That's up to you."

The way he said it, Levine was reminded that Stettin didn't want to break his hump over this one. Levine walked over to his desk and sat down and said, "I got two more names. From Casetta. Jake Mosca and Barney Feldman. No addresses. See what you can dig up on them, will you? And go talk to them."

"Sure. How was Casetta?"

"I don't know. Maybe Gold cheated him at poker. Maybe Gold was playing around with his wife. He didn't act nervous or worried." Levine rubbed a hand wearily across his face. "I'll go talk to Gold now," he said. "Did we get the M.E.'s report?"

"It's right there on your desk."

Levine didn't open it. He didn't want to read about Morry Gold's corpse. He said, "What kind of gun?"

"A thirty-eight. You look tired, Abe."

"I guess I am. I can sleep late tomorrow."

"Sure."

"Oh, one more thing. Elly Kapp isn't at that address any more. See what you can find there, will you?"

"Will do."

Levine walked down the hall again and took over the questioning of Gold. After Andrews and Campbell had left the room, Levine looked at Gold and said, "What did Morry do to you?"

Gold shook his head.

"You're a cautious man, Gold." Levine's voice rose impatiently. "It had to be something strong to make you kill him. Did he cheat you?"

Humor flickered at the corners of Gold's mouth. "He cheated me always," he said. "For years. I was used to it, Abraham."

Levine shrugged off the use of the first name. It wasn't important enough to be angry about. "So he was blackmailing you," he said, "and finally you'd had enough. But didn't you know someone would hear the sound of the shot? Mrs. Temple saw you go out."

"A false identification," said Gold. "I would risk nothing for Maurice. He was not worth the danger of killing him."

Levine shrugged. If Gold knew a potato silencer had been used, he hadn't mentioned it. Not that Levine had expected the trick to work. Tricks like that work only in the movies. And killers go to the movies, too.

Levine asked questions for over two hours. Sometimes Gold answered, and sometimes he didn't. As the time wore on, Levine grew more and more tired, more and more heavy and depressed, but Gold remained unchanged, displaying only the same solid patience.

Finally, at three-thirty, Levine told him he could leave. Gold thanked him, with muted sardonicism, and left. Levine went back down the hall to the squadroom.

There was a note from Stettin. Elly Kapp was being held

in a precinct in west Brooklyn. Last night, he'd been caught halfway through the window of a warehouse near the Brooklyn piers, and tomorrow morning he would be transferred downtown.

Levine phoned the precinct and got permission from the Lieutenant of Detectives there to come over and question the prisoner. Stettin had taken the Chevy, so Levine had to drive an unfamiliar car, newer and stiffer.

Kapp had very little useful to say. At first, he said, "Morry Gold? I ain't seen him since we took the fall. I'm a very superstitious guy, Mister. I don't go near anyone who is with me when a job goes sour. That guy by me is a jinx."

Levine questioned him further, wanting to know the names of other thieves with whom Gold had had dealings, whether or not Gold had been known to cheat thieves in the past, whether or not Kapp knew of anyone who harbored a grudge against Gold. Kapp pleaded ignorance for a while, and then gradually began to look crafty.

"Maybe I could help you out," he said finally. "I don't promise you nothing, but maybe I could. If we could work out maybe a deal?"

Levine shook his head, and left the room. Kapp called after him, but Levine didn't listen to what he was saying. Kapp didn't know anything; his information would be useless. He would implicate anybody, make up any kind of story he thought Levine wanted to hear, if it would help him get a lighter sentence for the attempted robbery of the warehouse.

It was four o'clock. Levine brought the unfamiliar car back to the precinct, signed out, and went home.

The third day of the case, Levine came to work at four in the afternoon, starting a three-day tour on the night shift. As usual, Stettin was already there when he arrived.

"Hi, Abe," Stettin greeted. "I talked to Feldman yesterday. He owns a grocery store in Brownsville. Like everybody else, he didn't know Morry Gold all that well. But he did give me a couple more names."

"Good," said Levine. He had been about to shrug out of his coat, but now he kept it on.

"One of them's a woman," said Stettin. "May Torasch. She was possibly Gold's girl friend. Feldman didn't know for sure."

"What about Feldman?"

"I don't think so, Abe. He and Gold just know each other from the old days, that's all."

"All right."

"I tried to see the other one, Jake Mosca, but he wasn't home."

"Maybe he'll be home now." Levine started to button his coat again.

Stettin said, "Want me to come along?"

Levine was going to say no, tell him to check out the other names he had, but then he changed his mind. Stettin would be his partner for a while, so they ought to start learning how to work together. Besides, Stettin was only half-hearted in this case, and he might miss something important. Levine wished he'd questioned the grocer himself.

"Come on along," Levine said.

Mosca lived way out Flatbush Avenue toward Floyd Bennett. There were old two-family houses out that way, in disrepair, and small apartment buildings that weren't quite tenements. It was in one of the latter that Mosca lived, on the second floor.

The hall was full of smells, and badly-lit. A small boy who needed a haircut stood down at the far end of the hall and watched them as Levine knocked on the door.

There were sounds of movement inside, but that was all. Levine knocked again, and this time a voice called, "Who is it?"

"Police," called Levine.

Inside, a bureau drawer opened, and Levine heard

cursing. His eyes widening, he jumped quickly to one side, away from the door, shouting, "Andy! Get out of the way!"

From inside, there were sounds like wood cracking, and a series of punched-out holes appeared in the door just as Stettin started to obey.

Levine was clawing on his hip for his gun. The shots, sounding like wood cracking, kept resounding in the apartment, and the holes kept appearing in the door. Plaster was breaking in small chunks in the opposite wall now.

The door was thin, and Levine could hear the clicking when the gun was empty and the man inside kept pulling the trigger. He stepped in front of the door, raised his foot, kicked it just under the knob. The lock splintered away and the door swung open. The man inside was goggle-eyed with rage and fear.

The instant the door came open he threw the empty gun at Levine and spun away for the window. Levine ducked and ran into the apartment, shouting to Mosca to stop. Mosca went over the sill headfirst, out onto the fire escape. Levine fired at him, trying to hit him in the leg, but the bullet went wild. But before he could fire again Mosca went clattering down the fire escape.

Levine got to the window in time to see the man reach the ground. He ran across the weedy back yard, over the wooden fence, and went dodging into a junkyard piled high with rusting parts of automobiles.

Levine was trying to do everything at once. He started out the window, then realized Mosca had too much of a head-start on him. Then he remembered Andy and, as he descended to the floor, he realized that Stettin hadn't followed him into the room and wondered why.

The moment he emerged into the hallway the reason became clear. Andy was lying on his side a yard from the door, his entire left shoulder drenched with blood and his knees drawn up sharply. He was no longer moving. Levine bent over him for an instant, then swung about, ran down the stairs and out to the Chevy and called in.

Everyone seemed to show up at once. Ambulance and patrolmen and detectives, suddenly filling the corridor. Lieutenant Barker, chief of the precinct's detective squad, came with the rest and stood looking down at Andy Stettin, his face cold with rage. He listened to Levine's report of what had happened, saying nothing until Levine had finished.

Then he said, "He may pull through, Abe. He still has a chance. You mustn't blame yourself for this."

Should I have been able to tell him? Levine wondered. *He was new, and I was more or less breaking him in, showing him the ropes, so shouldn't I have told him that when you hear the cursing, when you hear the bureau drawer opening, get away from the door?*

But how could I have told him everything, all the different things you learn? You learn by trial and error, the same as in any other walk of life. But here, sometimes, they only give you one error.

It isn't fair.

The apartment was swarming with police, and soon they found out why Mosca had fired eight times through the door. A shoebox in a closet was a quarter full of heroin, cut and capsuled, ready for the retail trade. Mosca had a record, but for theft, not for narcotics, so there was no way Levine and Stettin could have known.

For an hour or two, Levine was confused. The world swirled around him at a mad pace, but he couldn't really concentrate on any of it. People talked to him, and he answered one way and another, without really understanding what was being said to him or what he was replying. He walked in a shocked daze, not comprehending.

He came out of it back at the precinct. The entire detective squad was there, all the off-duty men having been called in, and Lieutenant Barker was talking to them. They filled the squadroom, sitting on the desks and leaning against the walls, and Lieutenant Barker stood facing them.

"We're going to get this Jake Mosca," he was saying. "We're going to get him because Andy Stettin is damn close to death. Do you know why we have to get a cop-killer? It's because the cop is a *symbol*. He's a symbol of the law, the most solid symbol of the law the average citizen ever sees. Our society is held together by law, and we cannot let the symbol of the law be treated with arrogance and contempt.

"I want the man who shot Stettin. You'll get to everyone this Mosca knows, every place he might think of going. You'll get him because Andy Stettin is dying — and he is a cop."

No, thought Levine, *that's wrong. Andy Stettin is a man, and that's why we have to get Jake Mosca. He was alive, and now he may die. He is a living human being, and that's why we have to get his would-be killer. There shouldn't be any other reasons, there shouldn't have to be any other reasons.*

But he didn't say anything.

Apparently, the Lieutenant could see that Levine was still dazed, because he had him switch with Rizzo, who was catching at the squadroom phone this tour. For the rest of the tour, Levine sat by the phone in the empty squadroom, and tried to understand.

Andrews and Campbell brought Mosca in a little after eleven. They'd found him hiding in a girl friend's apartment, and when they brought him in he was bruised and semi-conscious. Campbell explained he'd tried to resist arrest, and no one argued with him.

Levine joined the early part of the questioning, and got Mosca's alibi for the night Morry Gold was killed. He made four phone calls, and the alibi checked out. Jake Mosca had not murdered Morry Gold.

The fourth day, Levine again arrived at the precinct at four o'clock. He was scheduled to catch this tour, so he spent another eight hours at the telephone, and got nothing done on the Morry Gold killing. The fifth day, working alone now, he went on with the investigation.

May Torasch, the woman whose name Andy Stettin had

learned, worked in the credit department of a Brooklyn department store. Levine went to her apartment, on the fringe of Sunset, at seven o'clock, and found her home. She was another blowsy woman, reminding him strongly of Sal Casetta's wife. But she was affable, and seemed to want to help, though she assured Levine that she and Morry Gold had never been close friends.

"Face it," she said, "he was a bum. He wasn't going nowhere, so I never wasted much time on him."

She had seen Morry two days before his death; they'd gone to a bar off Flatbush Avenue and had a few drinks. But she hadn't gone back to his apartment with him. She hadn't been in the mood.

"I was kind of low that night," she said.

"Was Morry low?" Levine asked.

"No, not him. He was the same as ever. He'd talk about the weather all the time, and his lousy landlady. I wouldn't have gone out with him, but I was feeling so low I didn't want to go home."

She didn't have any idea who might have murdered him. "He was just a bum, just a small-timer. Nobody paid any attention to him." Nor could she add to the names of Gold's acquaintances.

From her apartment, Levine went to the bar where she and Morry had last been together. It was called *The Green Lantern,* and was nearly empty when Levine walked in shortly before nine. He showed his identification to the bartender and asked about Morry Gold. But the bartender knew very few of his customers by name.

"I might know this guy by sight," he explained, "But the name don't mean a thing." And the same was true of May Torasch.

There were still two more names on the list, Joe Whistler and Arnie Hendricks, the latter being the Arnie Sal Casetta had mentioned. Joe Whistler was another bartender, so Levine went looking for him first, and found him at work, tending bar in a place called *Robert's,* in Canarsie, not more than a dozen blocks from Levine's home.

Whistler knew Gold only casually, and could add nothing. Levine spent half an hour with him, and then went in search of Arnie Hendricks.

Arnie Hendricks was a small-time fight manager, originally from Detroit. He wasn't at home, and the gym where he usually hung out was closed this time of night. Levine went back to the precinct, sat down at his desk, and looked at his notes.

He had eight names relating to Morry Gold. There were one brother, one woman, and six casual friends. None of them had offered any reasons for Morry's murder, none of them had suggested any suspects who might have hated Morry enough to kill him, and none of them had given any real cause to be considered a suspect himself, with the possible exception of Abner Gold.

But the more Levine thought about Abner Gold, the more he was willing to go along with Andy Stettin's idea. The man was afraid of an investigation not because he had murdered his brother, but because he was afraid the police would be able to link him to his brother's traffic in stolen goods.

Eight names. One of them, Arnie Hendricks, was still an unknown, but the other seven had been dead ends.

Someone had murdered Morry Gold. Somewhere in the world, the murderer still lived. He had a name and a face; and he had a connection somehow with Morry Gold. And he was practically unsought. Of the hundreds of millions of human beings on the face of the earth, only one Abraham Levine, who had never known Morry Gold in life, was striving to find the man who had brought about Morry Gold's death.

After a while, wearily, he put his notes away and pecked out his daily report on one of the office Remingtons. Then it was midnight, and he went home. And that was when he got some good news from the hospital — Andy Stettin was going to live.

The sixth day, he went to the precinct, reported in, got the Chevy, and went out looking for Arnie Hendricks. He spent seven hours on it, stopping off only to eat, but he couldn't find Hendricks anywhere. People he talked to had seen Hendricks during the day, so the man wasn't in hiding, but Levine couldn't seem to catch up with him. It was suggested that Hendricks might be off at a poker game somewhere in Manhattan, but Levine couldn't find out exactly where the poker game was being held.

He got back to the precinct at eleven-thirty, and started typing out his daily report. There wasn't much to report. He'd looked for Hendricks, and had failed to find him. He would look again tomorrow.

Lieutenant Barker came in at a quarter to twelve. That was unusual; the Lieutenant was rarely around later than eight or nine at night, unless something really important had happened in the precinct. He came into the squadroom and said, "Abe, can I talk to you? Bring that report along."

Levine pulled the incomplete report from the typewriter and followed the Lieutenant into his ofice. The Lieutenant sat down, and motioned for Levine to do the same, then held out his hand.

"Could I see that report?" he asked.

"It isn't finished."

"That's all right."

The Lieutenant glanced at the report, and then dropped it on his desk. "Abe," he said, "do you know what our full complement is supposed to be?"

"Twenty men, isn't it?"

"Right. And we have fifteen. With Crawley out, fourteen. Abe, here's your reports for the last six days. What have you been doing, man? We're understaffed, we're having trouble keeping up with the necessary stuff, and look what you've been doing. For six days you've been running around in circles. And for what? For a small-time punk who got a small-time punk's end."

"He was murdered, Lieutenant."

"Lots of people are murdered, Abe. When we can, we find out who did the job, and we turn him over to the DA. But we don't make an obsession out of it. Abe, for almost a week now you haven't been pulling your weight around here. There've been three complaints about how long it took us to respond to urgent calls. We're understaffed, but we're not *that* understaffed."

Barker tapped the little pile of reports. "This man Gold was a fence, and a cheap crook. He isn't worth it, Abe. We can't waste any more time on him. When you finish up this report, I want you to recommend we switch the case to Pending. And tomorrow I want you to get back with the team."

"Lieutenant, I've got one more man to —— "

"And tomorrow there'll be one more, and the day after that one more. Abe, you've been working on nothing else at *all*. Forget it, will you? This is a cheap penny-ante bum. Even his brother doesn't care who killed him. Let it go, Abe."

He leaned forward over the desk. "Abe, some cases don't get solved right away. That's what the Pending file is for. So six weeks from now, or six months from now, or six years from now, while we're working on something else, when the break finally does come, we can pull that case out and hit it hot and heavy again. But it's *cold* now, Abe, so let it lie."

Speeches roiled around inside Levine's head, but they were only words so he didn't say them. He nodded, reluctantly. "Yes, sir," he said.

"The man was a bum," said the Lieutenant, "pure and simple. Forget him, he isn't worth your time."

"Yes, sir," said Levine.

He went back to the squadroom and finished typing the

report, recommending that the Morry Gold case be switched to the Pending file. Then it was twelve o'clock, and he left the precinct and walked to the subway station. The underground platform was cold and deserted. He stood shivering on the concrete, his hands jammed deep into his pockets. He waited twenty minutes before a train came. Then it did come, crashed into the station and squealed to a stop. The doors in front of Levine slid back with no hands touching them, and he stepped aboard.

The car was empty, with a few newspapers abandoned on the seats. The doors slid shut behind him and the train started forward. He was the only one in the car. He was the only one in the car and all the seats were empty, but he didn't sit down.

The train rocked and jolted as it hurtled through the cold hole under Brooklyn, and Abraham Levine stood swaying in the middle of the empty car, a short man, bulky in his overcoat, hulk-shouldered, crying.

AFTER I'M GONE

Afternoon visiting hours at the hospital were from two till five, so when Detective Abraham Levine of Brooklyn's Forty-Third Precinct got off his tour at four P.M. he took a Rockaway Parkway bus to the hospital and spent thirty-five minutes with Detective Andy Stettin. Levine and Andy had been together when Andy was hit, a bullet high on the left side of the chest, fired through a closed door. Andy, a promising youngster, a hotshot, one of the new breed of college cops, had been close to death for a while, but was now on the mend, and very bored and impatient with hospital routine.

It wasn't really necessary for Levine to go through this ritual every day, nor did he have that much to say to the youngster, and in fact he knew full well he was only doing it because he so much didn't want to. There was a certain amount of guilt involved, since Levine was secretly happy that the bullet had ended his brief partnership with Andy

Stettin, but in truth Andy wasn't the main point here at all. The main point was the hospital.

To Andy Stettin, a young fellow, healthy and self-assured, the hospital was merely a nuisance and a bore. To Abraham Levine, fifty-three years of age, short and stocky, overweight and short of wind, with a tired heart that skipped the occasional beat, the hospital was a horrible presentiment, an all-too-possible future. Those sad withered men, shrunken within their maroon or brown robes, shuffling down the wide featureless corridors in their Christmas-present slippers, were a potential tomorrow that could be very close indeed. Going to the hospital every afternoon was for Levine a painful repeated confrontation with his own worst fears.

Today, a Thursday, Levine told Andy that there continued to be no break in the case of Maurice Gold, during the investigation of whose murder Andy had been shot, by a drug dealer who unfortunately was not Gold's killer. Andy shrugged, not really interested: "Gold is gonna stay Open," he said.

Levine had to agree. With some sort of reverse logic, when a case became inactive the Police Department phrase was that it was Opened. "Open that," meant in reality to close it, to cease to work on it. The reason behind the Newspeak phraseology was that only an arrest could Close a case; an inactive case could always be reactivated by fresh evidence, and therefore it would remain — unto eternity, most likely — Open.

Levine and Andy also talked awhile about Levine's regular partner, Jack Crawley, a big shambling mean-looking harness bull with whom Levine had a very easy and reassuring relationship. Crawley had just come back on duty this week after his convalescent leave — he had been, several months ago, shot in the leg — and the long spell of inactivity had made him more bristly and bad-tempered than ever. "I think he'll arrest *me* pretty soon," Levine said.

Andy laughed at that, but what he mostly wanted to talk about was a nurse he had his eye on, a pretty young thing, very short and compact, squeezed into a too-tight uniform. Both times the girl passed by while Levine was there, Andy did some elephantine flirting, very heavy-handed arch remarks that Levine found embarrassing but which the girl appeared to enjoy. The second time, after both men had watched the provocative departure of the nurse, Andy grinned and said, "The sap still rises, eh, Abe?"

"The sap also sets," Levine told him, getting to his feet. "See you tomorrow, Andy."

"Thanks for coming by."

Levine was walking down the wide corridor, not meeting the eyes of the ambulatory patients, when a hand touched his elbow and a gravelly voice said, quietly, "Let's just walk around here a while."

Surprised, Levine looked to his right and saw a short, blocky, pugnacious-looking man of about his own age, wearing an expensive topcoat open over a rather wrinkled suit, and an old-fashioned snap-brim hat pulled low enough to make it difficult to see his eyes. Levine noticed the awkward bunchiness of the man's tie-knot, as though he had got himself up in costume like a trick-or-treater, as though his real persona existed in some other mode.

The man gave Levine a quick sidelong glance from under his hatbrim. His hand held firmly to Levine's elbow. "You're a cop, right? Abraham Levine, detective. Visiting the cop in there."

"Yes?"

"So let's talk a little bit."

They had reached an intersection of corridors. The elevators were straight ahead, but the man was pulling Levine to the right. "Talk about what?" Levine asked, trying to shake loose.

"Cops and robbers," the man said. "I got a proposition."

Levine planted his feet, refusing to move. Peeling the

man's fingers from his elbow, he said, "What sort of proposition?"

With darting movements of his head, the man shot wary glances along the corridors. "I don't like it here," he said. "Exposed here."

"Exposed to what?"

"Listen," the man said, moving closer, his breath warm on Levine's chin, his hatbrim nearly touching Levine's face. "You know Giacomo Polito," he said.

"I know who he is. Mafia chieftan. He controls one of the five families."

"I'm a soldier for him," the man said, his voice low but harsh, pushing with intensity. "I know Giacomo's whole life story."

Levine frowned, trying to see this too-close face, read meaning into the tone of the husky tense voice. Was this an offer of information? The setting was unusual, the manner odd, but what else could it be? Levine said, "You want to sell that life story?"

"Don't rush me." Another darting glance. "Giacomo disappeared my son," the man said, still in the same breathy way. "He knows I know."

"Ah."

"You take your bus, like you do," the man said. "Look out the back window. When you see a green Buick following, you get off the bus. There's a—kind of a flower on the aerial."

"And who are you?" Levine asked him. "What's your name?"

"What's the dif? Call me Bobby."

"Bobby?" The incongruity of that name with this man made Levine smile despite himself.

The man looked up, facing Levine more directly than before. He too smiled, but with an edge to it. "That was my son's name," he said.

The green Buick with the red plastic chrysanthemum taped to its antenna followed the bus for a dozen blocks before Levine decided to follow through. Then he got off at the next stop, stood at the curb while the bus drove off, and waited for the Buick to stop in front of him.

The delay had been because Levine wasn't entirely sure what he thought of "Bobby" and his story. A Mafia soldier who decided to defect usually did so when under indictment himself for some major crime, when he could trade his knowledge for softer treatment from the courts. Simple revenge between criminals rarely included squealing to the police. If Bobby's son had been killed by Giacomo Polito, in the normal course of events Bobby would simply kill Polito, or be himself killed in the attempt. The Mafia tended to run very much along the lines of a Shakespearian tragedy, with few roles for outsiders.

In addition, if Bobby had decided that *his* vengeance required selling Polito to the police, why not do it the simple normal way? Why not simply drive to Manhattan and go to the Organized Crime Unit in Police Headquarters and make his deal there? Why talk to some obscure precinct detective in the depths of Brooklyn, and in particular why do it in a hospital corridor? And why all this counterspy huggermugger?

What finally decided Levine to take the next step was that he couldn't think of any rational alternative explanation for Bobby's actions. If someone had decided to murder Levine, of course, this would be an excellent ploy to put him in a position where it could be done; but Levine could think of no one at the moment who would have a motive. He wasn't due to be a witness in any upcoming trials, he hadn't made any potentially dangerous arrests recently, nor had he received notification within the last year or so of any felons, arrested by himself, who had been released from prison. Also, if Bobby's story were merely a charade for some sort of con game, how could it hurt Levine? He wouldn't pay anything or sign anything or even necessarily believe anything. And finally, there had been the real brimstone aura of truth in that last direct stare from Bobby, when he'd said, "That was my son's name."

So for all those reasons Levine had ultimately stepped off the bus and stood waiting until the Buick pulled to a stop in front of him. But, before getting into the car, he did nevertheless check the floor behind the front seat, just to be absolutely certain there was no one crouched back there, with a pistol or a knife or a length of wire.

There was nothing; just some empty beer cans. So Levine opened the front passenger door and bent to enter the car, but Bobby was leaning over toward him from the steering wheel, saying, "Uh, would you take down the — get rid of the flower?"

"Of course."

Masking tape had been wrapped around both antenna and flower stalk; Levine tugged on the plastic stalk and the tape ripped, releasing it. He then got into the car and shut the door, feeling vaguely foolish to be sitting here with a red flower in his lap. He tossed it stop the dashboard as Bobby accelerated away from the curb, checking both the inside and outside mirrors, saying, "I did shake 'em, but you never know."

"You're being followed?"

"Oh, sure," he said, shrugging as though it were an everyday event. "They wanna know I'm not going anywhere before the big day."

"What big day?"

"Wipe out," Bobby said, and ran a finger along his neck. "Giacomo's got a contract out on me."

"You're sure of that?"

Bobby gave him a quick glance, almost of contempt, then went back to his fitful concentration on the road ahead and both mirrors. "I'm sure of everything," he said. "When I'm not sure, I shut up."

"So you want police protection, is that it?"

"Why don't *I* tell *you* what I want, okay?"

Levine smiled at the rebuff. "Okay," he said.

Bobby turned a corner. He seemed to be driving at random, though trending northwest, away from the hospital and in the general direction of Manhattan, several miles away. "Giacomo's got a young wife," he said. "The old Mama died, all over cancer, right? So Giacomo went to Vegas to work out his grief, he come back with a bride. A dancer at the Aladdin, calls herself Terri. With an I."

"Uh huh."

"My son —— "

"Bobby."

"My *son*. Got hooked on this Terri. He was like a dog, there's a bitch in the neighborhood in heat, you cannot keep that dog in the house."

"Dangerous."

"She says he raped her," Bobby said. "He didn't rape her, she was asking for it."

Levine kept silent. He watched Bobby's fingers twitch and fidget on the steering wheel.

"A bodyguard found them at it," Bobby said. "Naturally she had to cry rape. My son told his story, the bodyguard said forget it, my son went home. Terri with the I, she went to Giacomo. She talked to Giacomo, but Giacomo didn't talk to nobody, not to me, not to my son, not to nobody. The bodyguard got disappeared. My son got disappeared. I said, 'Giacomo, we know one another a long time, why don't you talk to me first, ask me a question?' He still don't talk. I go away, and he puts a contract on me, he puts shadows on me to be sure I'm still here for the hit."

"There's a special time for the . . . hit?"

"Saturday night. Day after tomorrow. I still got friends to

whisper me things. At Barolli's Seafood House in Far Rockaway, upstairs in the private dining room, there's gonna be a banquet. It's Giacomo's first wedding anniversary." Bobby spoke the words with no apparent irony. "That's where they're gonna take me out. By the time they're at the coffee and cigars, I'm at the bottom of Jamaica Bay."

"Pretty."

"Businesslike," Bobby said.

"If it's police protection you want — "

Levine was stopped by Bobby's cold eyes looking directly at him. "You gonna explain life to me, Mr. Levine?"

"Sorry."

"I know about police protection," Bobby said. He lifted his right hand from the steering wheel and rubbed his thumb back and forth over the pads of his other fingers. "With this hand," he said, "I have paid protective police to be blind and deaf while the subject of their concern was falling out a window. You are an honest cop, Mr. Levine, and that's very nice, that's why you and me are talking, but let me break you the sad news. There are one or two rotten apples in your crowd."

"I know that."

"I also know about the Feds and their witness protection plan," Bobby said. "They will give me a new name, a new house in a new city, a new job, a new driver's license, a whole entire new life."

"That's right."

"All they take away is my old life," Bobby said. "That's what Giacomo has in mind, too. I *like* my old life."

"So far," Levine said, "I'm not sure why you're telling me all this."

"Because I have a scheme," Bobby said, "but my scheme is taking too long. I won't be able to leave town until the middle of next week. I'm okay until Saturday, but when I don't show at the celebration they'll start looking for me. It'll be tougher for me to move around town."

"I can see that."

"I need a courier," Bobby said. "I need protection and assistance. I need an honest cop to run my errands and see that nobody offs me."

"Tell me your scheme," Levine said.

"I am assembling information," Bobby told him. "I am talking into a tape recorder, I am giving facts and names and dates, I am nailing Giacomo to the cross. And I am getting the physical evidence, too, the contracts and the photos and the letters and the wiretaps and everything else."

"Giacomo shouldn't have killed your son," Levine said.

"Not without talking to me."

"You'll turn over all this information next week?"

"To the law?" Bobby grinned, a kind of distorted grimace that created deep crevices in his cheeks. "You got the wrong idea," he said.

"Then who do you give it all to, all these proofs and information?"

"Giacomo's partners," Bobby said. "His friends. His fellow *capi*. His business associates. What I'm putting together is what he's done to *them* over the years. I have stuff Giacomo himself can't remember. I have enough to get him offed ten times from ten different people."

"I see," Levine said. "You ruin Giacomo with the mob, and his contract on you ceases to matter."

"*And* he's dead. And the Terri with him."

"Why do you think I would help you?" Levine asked.

Again the wrenching grin. "Because I'm gonna give you some scraps from my table," Bobby said. "Just a few things you'd like to know."

"About Giacomo."

"Who else?" Under the wide-brimmed hat, under the darting, dashing anxious eyes, Bobby smiled like a death's head. "Just enough to put Giacomo in prison," he said. "Where it'll be easier for his friends to kill him."

For forty minutes Levine sat at Lieutenant Barker's desk and looked at pictures, front and side views of Caucasian males, page after page of tough guys behind clear plastic. The infinite variety of human appearance became confined here to variations on one theme: the Beast, without Beauty.

"Him," Levine said.

Inspector Santangelo leaned over Levine's shoulder and whistled. "You sure?"

"That's him, all right."

It was Bobby, no question. Without the hat, he was shown to have a low broad forehead, thick pepper-and-salt hair that grew spikily across his head, and cold eyes that seemed to slink and lurk behind half-lowered lids. Without the hat he looked more like a snake. The name under the photos was *Ralph Banadando*.

Inspector Santangelo was visibly impressed. Crossing the lieutenant's office to resume his seat on the sofa, he said, "No wonder he knows where the bodies are buried. And no wonder he called Polito by his first name."

Lieutenant Barker, chief of the precinct's detective squad, whose office this was, said, "Who is he?"

"Benny Banadando," the inspector said. "He's Giacomo Polito's righthand man, they came up through the ranks together. He's the number two man in that mob." Grinning at Levine, he said, "That's no soldier. He told you he was a soldier? That's a General." Nodding at Barker, seated in what was usually the visitor's chair, he said, "You did right to call me, Fred."

"Thanks."

It was Friday morning, nearly noon. Yesterday, saying he would get in touch with Levine sometime today to hear his answer, whether or not he would accept the proposition, Bobby—Ralph "Benny" Banadando, now—had let Levine off six blocks from his home, giving Levine ten minutes to walk and think. At home, he had at once phoned the precinct to give Lieutenant Barker a brief recap of the conversation. Given the truth of Bobby's remark about the "one or two rotten apples" in the Police Department, they'd agreed not to spread the story very widely, and Barker had phoned his old friend Inspector Santangelo, now assigned to the Organized Crime Unit. This morning Santangelo had come down to the Forty-Third Precinct with his book of mug shots, and now Levine had a name for Bobby. He said, "Does Banadando have a son?"

"He did," Santangelo said in a dry tone. "Fellow named Robert, not very sweet. What do you want to do, Abe? Can I call you Abe?"

"Sure."

"And I'm Mike," Santangelo said. "You want to turn this thing over to me, or do you want to follow through yourself?"

"You mean, do I want to tell Banadando yes or no."

"That's what I mean." Grinning at some private thought, Santangelo sat back on the sofa, stretching his long legs in the small office. "Before you answer," he said, "let me say this. I don't want to bring this news back to my shop, because if I do it'll get to Polito and he won't wait for the symbolic moment of his anniversary dinner."

Levine nodded. "That's what we thought, too."

"In addition," Santangelo said, "you'll be marked yourself, Abe, because Polito won't be sure how much Banadando told you."

Lieutenant Barker said, "He won't try to kill a cop."

"Probably not," Santangelo said. "But if he's nervous enough, it's a possibility. From our point of view, it's better if Banadando can work his scheme in peace and quiet. But what that means, Abe, we can't provide backup."

"I can," Lieutenant Barker said. "Abe's partner, Jack Crawley, can back him up."

"That's not quite the same as three busloads of TPF,"

Santangelo said. "You see what I'm getting at, Abe? This could be dangerous for you."

"What happens if I tell Banadando no?"

"I pull him in," Santangelo said. "I try to convince him his scheme is busted anyway and he might as well cooperate with us."

"He'll say no."

Santangelo shrugged. "It's worth a try."

Levine said, "You won't have to. I'll tell him yes."

"Good," said Banadando's husky, low, insinuating voice on the phone. It was twenty to five on Friday afternoon and Levine was in the hospital again, visiting with Andy Stettin. Andy's phone had rung and it was Banadando, for Levine.

Conscious of Andy's curious eyes on him, Levine said into the phone, "What happens now?"

"Nothing. I can still play my own hand till tomorrow night. You know Long Island well?"

"Pretty well."

"About fifty miles out there's a town called Bay Shore. On the Great South Bay."

"I know it."

"Go there Sunday morning, around nine. Go down to the end of Maple, park there."

"What will I —— " But Banadando had hung up.

Levine replaced the receiver and Andy said, "What was that? Sounded like a real sweetheart."

"Mobster," Levine said. "He's gonna give some evidence, for some reason he made me the intermediary."

"Why's he giving evidence?"

Levine was reluctant to hold back — it wasn't as though he mistrusted *Andy* — but he had to maintain a habit of reticence in this situation. "Some of his pals have a contract on him," he said.

Andy's lip curled. "Let 'em kill each other off. Best thing that can happen." ·

"I suppose so," said Levine slowly, but the words were ashes in his mouth. He understood why what Andy had just said was the common, almost the universal belief among the police; whenever one mobster killed another, great smiles of happiness lit up the faces in the precinct houses. But Levine just couldn't take pleasure from the death of a human being, no matter who, no matter what he had done in his life. He supposed it was really selfishness, really only a matter of projecting their deaths onto himself, visualizing his own end in theirs, that made him troubled and sad at the cutting short of lives so stained and spoiled, but nevertheless he just couldn't bring himself to share in the general glee at the thought of a murdered mobster.

A little later, as he was leaving Andy's room, he paused in the doorway to let a wizened ancient man pass by, moving slowly and awkwardly and painfully with the help of a walker. *That's me,* Levine thought, and behind him Andy said, "If they start bumping one another off, Abe, just step to one side."

Levine looked back at him, bewildered, his mind for an instant filling with visions of doddering oldsters bumping one another off: "What do you mean?"

"Your mobster pals. They love to kill so much, let 'em kill each other. It isn't up to us to stop it, or to get in the way."

"I'll stay out of the way," Levine promised. Then he smiled and waved and left, walking around the ancient man, who had barely progressed beyond the doorway.

Maple Avenue in Bay Shore ended on a long wide dock, covered with asphalt and its center lined with parking meters. Levine found a free meter, got out of the car, and strolled a bit, smelling the salt tang. Once or twice he glanced back the way he had come, without seeing Jack Crawley; which was as it should be.

Out near the end of the dock, several small boats were offloading bushel baskets and burlap bags, all filled with clams. Two trucks were receiving the harvest, and the men working there called cheerfully at one another, talking more loudly than necessary, but apparently filled with high spirits because of the clarity and beauty of the day.

Nine A.M. on the third Sunday in October. The air was clear, the sun bright in a sky dotted with clouds, the water frisky and glinting and cold-looking. Levine inhaled deeply, glad to be alive, barely even conscious of the straps around his shoulders and chest, under his shirt, holding the recording apparatus.

He strolled aimlessly on the dock for about fifteen minutes and then turned at the sound of a *beep-beep* to see a small inboard motorboat bobbing next to the dock, with Banadando at the wheel. Banadando gestured, and Levine crossed over to stand looking down at him. "Come aboard," Banadando said. "We'll go for a run on the bay."

Clammers and fishermen were in other small boats dotting the bay. Long Island was five miles or so to the north, the barrier beach called Fire Island was just to the south, and Banadando's boat—*Bobby's Dream* was the name painted on the stern in flowing golden letters—was simply another anonymous speck on the dancing water.

Bobby's Dream was compact but comfortable, its cabin—where Levine now sat—containing a tiny galley-style kitchen, cunning storage spaces, a foldaway table and a pair of long upholstered benches that converted to twin beds. "Nice, huh?" Banadando said, coming down into the cabin after cutting the engine and dropping anchor.

"Very clever," Levine said.

"That, too," Banadando agreed. Today he wore a longbilled white yachting cap edged in gold, the bill shielding his eyes as yesterday's hat had done. In blue blazer, white scarf and white pants, he was almost a parody of the weekend yachtsman. Sitting on the bench across from Levine, he said, "After dark I take the inlet, I go out to the ocean, I sleep in comfort and safety. Nobody knows where I am or where I'll be next. I land where I want, when I want. Until I leave town, this is the safest place in the world for me."

"I can see that," Levine said.

"You wired?"

"Of course," Levine said.

Banadando shook his head, smirking a bit. "We all go through the motions, right? You know I know you're gonna be wired, so I know you know I won't say anything you can use. But still you got to go through the whole thing, strap it on, walk around like a telephone company employee. You broadcasting or taping?"

"Taping," Levine said, wondering if Banadando would insist on being given the tape.

But Banadando merely smiled, saying, "Good. If you were broadcasting, we'd be too far out for your backup to read."

"That's right. Mr. Banadando, we——"

Banadando made a face. "I figured you'd find that out, who I am, but I don't like it. How many cops know about our little conversation?"

"Four, including me. We're already aware of the existence of rotten apples. Don't worry, we won't alert Polito through the department."

"Don't tell me not to worry, Mr. Levine."

"Sorry."

"You're a long time dead."

"I agree," Levine said.

Banadando took from an outside pocket of his blazer a sheet of white typewriter paper folded into quarters. Opening this, smoothing it on the tabletop, he turned it so the handwriting faced Levine. It was large block-printed letters in black ink. He said, "You see all this?"

"Yes?"

"I'm not giving you this paper, you're remembering it. Or you'll listen to your tape, later. You see what I mean?"

Levine looked at him. "Why do you think I'm going to be in that much trouble, Mr. Banadando?"

"Because I don't know how smart you are," Banadando said. "Maybe you're very dumb. Maybe one of the three cops you talked to is right now on the phone to Giacomo. Maybe you get nervous in the clutch. Maybe all kinds of things. I can't see the future, Mr. Levine, so I protect myself from it just as hard as I can. Okay?"

"Okay," Levine said.

Banadando's fingertip touched the first word on the sheet of paper. His hands were thick and stubby-fingered, but very clean, with meticulously-groomed nails. The effect, however, was not of cleanliness but of a kind of doughy unhealthfulness. "This," Banadando said, his sausage finger tapping the word, "is a telephone number."

Levine frowned. The word, all alone near the top of the sheet, was THIRSTY. "It is?"

"The phone dial doesn't just have numbers," Banadando reminded him. "It has letters. Dial those letters. You'll call just after noon today; this is back in the city, it's a city number."

"All right."

"You got to call no later than ten past twelve, or he won't be there."

"All right."

"When the guy answers, you tell him you're Abe. That's all he knows about you, that's all he needs to know. He'll tell you does he have the stuff yet or not. If it's no, he'll tell you when to call again."

"What is this stuff?"

"Let it be a surprise," Banadando said.

Levine took a breath. "Mr. Banadando," he said, "I have to tell you something you should already know. If any evidence of crime is put in my possession, I am going to turn it over to my superiors."

"Sure you are," Banadando said. "You'll take the package,

you'll sniff all over it like a bird-dog, you'll get nothing out of it. The next thing that happens, you'll bring it to me."

"But you realize we'll study it first."

"I am not here to be stupid," Banadando said. His finger moved down to the next item, below THIRSTY. There was the word KOPYKAT, and under it an address: 1411 BROADWAY. "This is a copying service," he said. "It's a chain, there's Kopykats all over the city. This is the Broadway one, you got it?"

"Yes."

"They're open on Sunday. This afternoon, any time this afternoon, you go there and pick up the package for Mr. Robert. If there's no package, don't worry about it."

"All right."

The stubby finger moved down to the last item on the sheet of paper: BELLPORT on one line, and under it HOWELL'S POINT. "Tomorrow morning," he said. "It's farther out from the city, so let's say ten o'clock. You bring me the Kopykat package and the other package, and I tell you what next."

"And the scraps from your table?"

With a thin smile, Banadando shook his head. "We pay at the end," he said.

"No," Levine said. "We have to have something now, to prove it's worthwhile."

Banadando sat back, brooding. The small movements of the boats were comforting at first, but then insistent. A large white ferry went by, on its way to Fire Island, and its wake made the *Bobby's Dream* heave on the water, like something alive and in pain.

"Upstate in Attica," Banadando said at last, "in the state pen there, you got a guy named Johnson, serving five consecutive life terms. He's never coming out. He'll be the only Johnson there with that sentence."

Levine smiled faintly. "I guess you're right."

"In Vermont," Banadando said, speaking slowly, picking

his words with obvious care, "there used to be a ski lodge called TransAlpine, had a big Olympic indoor skating rink. Burned down. No link between that and Johnson at all, right?"

"You tell me," Levine said.

"Johnson did things for Giacomo sometimes," Banadando said. "Giacomo had a piece of TransAlpine. Not right out in front, but you could find it."

"And?"

"Johnson hired the torch."

"It was arson?"

"Nobody ever said it was," Banadando said. "Not up there in Vermont. All I say to you is, Johnson hired the torch. Johnson and TransAlpine, there's no link there, so nobody ever talked to Johnson about that. Now all of a sudden I'm giving you a link. And what has Johnson got to lose?"

"The same as the rest of us," Levine said.

The man who answered the Thirsty phone number had a thin raspy voice. He said, "I got everything but the gun. You want?"

"Yes," Levine said.

"In Manhattan," the raspy voice said, "79th Street and Broadway, there's benches at the median, middle of the street, where people sit in the sun. Around two o'clock there'll be an old guy there with the package, gift-wrapped. Tell him you're Abe."

Levine followed directions and found half a dozen elderly men on the stone bench there, faces turned to the thin clear autumn sun. The faces were absorbing the gold, hoarding it, stocking it up for the long cold time in the dark to come.

One of the old men held in his lap a parcel that looked like a box of candy gaily wrapped in Happy Birthday paper. Levine went to him, identified himself as Abe, and took delivery. When Levine asked him how he'd come by the package, the old man said, "Fella gave it to me half an hour ago with a five dollar bill. Said you'd be along, said he couldn't wait, said I had an honest face."

The next old man over laughed, showing a mouth without teeth. "I said to the fella," he announced, "what kinda face you think *I* got? Paid me no never mind."

Carrying the Happy Birthday parcel, Levine went down Broadway to Kopykat, where he picked up the package for Mr. Robert. Then he continued on downtown to hand the material over to Inspector Santangelo at the Organized Crime Unit. "People upstate are talking to Johnson," Santangelo said.

"But is he talking to them?"

Santangelo grinned. "He will."

The next morning, Santangelo brought the two packages to the Forty-Third Precinct and handed them back to Levine in Lieutenant Barker's office. The Kopykat package had turned out to be copies of about forty ledger pages, but only numbers and abbreviations were filled in, making it useless by itself; you'd have to know what business those pages were connected to, and presumably Banadando's intended customer would know.

As for the birthday present, that box had contained a jumble of sales slips, for items ranging from automobiles and furs to coffee tables and refrigerators, plus a bunch of photos and negatives. There were a dozen pictures of what appeared to be the same orgy, there were pictures of a man getting into a car on a city street, pictures of a man at a construction site, of a truck being loaded or unloaded at the same site, of two men exchanging an envelope in the doorway of an appliance store.

Everything had been fingerprinted and photographed and brooded over, but there wasn't so far much value in this material. "It's puzzle parts," Santangelo said. "Just a couple stray puzzle parts. Banadando has the rest."

Monday was a less pretty day than Sunday had been, the broad sky piling up with tumbled dirty clouds and a damp breeze blowing from the northeast. With Banadando's packages on the front seat beside him, Levine drove out the Long Island Expressway and took the turnoff south for Bellport. He found Howell's Point, left the car, and saw Banadando approaching on a bicycle, dressed in his yachting outfit, with a supermarket bag in the basket. Banadando looked unexpectedly human and vulnerable, not at all like the tough guy he really was. Levine was pleased with the man, almost proud of him, for how matter-of-factly he carried it off.

Dismounting, Banadando said, "Take the groceries, okay? The boat's just over here."

Banadando walked the bike, and Levine followed with the bag and the two packages. The bag contained milk, tomatoes, lettuce, English muffins, a steak. Levine found himself wondering: Does Banadando have a wife? Is she part of his escape plan, or is he abandoning her, or does she not exist? Maybe she's already gone on ahead to prepare their next home. Banadando's style was that of the complete loner, but on the other hand he was only involved in this problem because of his emotional attachment to his son.

That was why Levine had never been able to go along with the idea that a murdered mobster was something to be happy about. Even the worst of human beings was still in some way a human being, was more than and other than a simple cartoon criminal. No death should be gloated over.

Aboard the boat, Banadando lashed the bike to the foredeck, then cast them off and headed out onto the bay, while Levine went below and put away the groceries. Coming up again on deck, where Banadando sat in a tall canvas chair at the wheel, steering them on a long gradual curve eastward into Bellport Bay, Levine said, "I'm not wired today. Thought you'd like to know."

Banadando grinned at him. "Waste of good tape, huh?"

"You won't say anything useful while I'm recording you."

"I won't say anything useful at all. Not the way you mean."

They ran southeast for fifteen minutes, then Banadando dropped anchor near Ridge Island and they went below together to talk. Levine explained that the Thirsty man had said he had everything but the gun, and Banadando waved that away: "I don't need the gun. I got enough without the gun."

"Well, here it all is," Levine said, gesturing to the two packages on the table.

Banadando nodded at the packages and grinned. "Made no sense to you, huh?"

"That's right."

"It'll make sense to some people," Banadando said. "And that's all it has to do. What about Johnson?"

"He's being talked to."

"He'll be very interesting, Johnson. Okay, time to memorize."

It was another sheet of paper, instructions on another two pick-ups. Levine listened and nodded, and when Banadando was done he said, "How long am I your messenger?"

"Two more days," Banadando said. "Tomorrow morning, you bring me this stuff, I give you the last shopping list. Wednesday morning, you bring me the last of it, I give you a nice package for yourself. The Johnson stuff is just a teaser; Wednesday morning I give you a banquet."

"And you leave."

"That's right," Banadando said. "And if you keep your ear to the ground the next few months, Detective Levine, you will hear some far-away explosions."

Their business done, they both went up on deck, and Levine sat in the second canvas chair while Banadando steered back toward Bellport. Even though the sky was lowering with clouds and there was a chill dampness in the air, there was something extraordinarily pleasant about being out here in this boat, skimming the choppy little wavelets, far from the cares of the world.

Not far enough. They were almost to Howell's Point, Levine could actually see his own car and a few other cars and some people walking along the pier when Banadando suddenly swore and spun the wheel and the *Bobby's Dream* veered around in a tight half-circle, lying way over on its side into the turn, spewing foam in a great white welt on the gray water.

It wasn't till they were far from shore, out in the empty middle of the bay, that Banadando slowed the boat again and Levine could talk to him, saying, "Friends of yours back there?"

"Friends of *his*," Banadando said, his voice vibrating like a guitar string. Tension had bunched the muscles in his cheeks and around his mouth, and his lips were thin and bloodless.

Levine said, "I wasn't followed, I can tell you that. My back-up would have known."

"The supermarket," Banadando said. "I can't even go to the supermarket. This is *rotten* luck, *rotten* luck."

"Now he knows about the boat."

"He can put people all around this bay, Giacomo can," Banadando said. "If he knows there's a reason. And now he knows there's a reason."

"I'll just mention police protection once," Levine said.

Banadando nodded. "Good," he said. "That was the mention. Look here."

From an enclosed cabinet under the wheel, Banadando pulled out a Defense Mapping Agency book of Sailing Directions, found the pages he wanted, and showed Levine what he intended to do. "Long Island's a hundred twenty miles long," he said. "From where we are here, there's like another seventy miles out to the end. But I can't stay on the South Shore any more, so here's what I'm gonna do. I don't have to go all the way out to Montauk Point at the end of the island. Here by Hampton Bays I can take the Shinnecock Canal through to Peconic Bay, then I only have to go out around Orient Point and there I am on the North Shore. Then I head west again, across Long Island Sound. Look here on this map, west of Mattituck Inlet, you see this little dip in the coastline?"

"Yes."

"There's a dirt road there, comes down from Bergen Avenue. I know that place from years ago. There's a little wooden dock there, that's all. Nobody around. That's where we meet tomorrow, let Giacomo and his boys search the South Shore all they want."

Looking at the maps, Levine said, "That's a long way to go, in a small boat like that."

"A hundred miles," Banadando said, dismissing it. "Maybe less. Don't worry, Levine, I'll be there. Between now and Wednesday, let's face it, the only way I stay alive is to do things Giacomo thinks I won't do or can't do."

"You're right," Levine said.

"I'm always right," Banadando said. "I can't take you back to your car. I'll drop you at Center Moriches, you can take a cab back."

Levine made that day's pick-ups with no trouble, and that evening, as rain tapped hesitantly at the windows, the four policemen who knew about Banadando—being Levine and Jack Crawley and Lieutenant Barker and Inspector Santangelo—met in the lieutenant's office at the precinct to decide what to do next.

Jack Crawley, a big beefy man with heavy shoulders and hands and a generally dissatisfied look, had no doubt what *he* wanted to do next: "Bring in everybody," he said. "Inspector, you bring in your whole Organized Crime Unit, we bring in plainclothes *and* uniformed people from the precinct, and we surround that mother. I don't want Abe to spend any more time in the middle of some other clown's argument."

"I'm already in, Jack," Levine said. "We're on the verge of getting some very useful information. I think Banadando actually is as smart as he thinks he is, and that he'll manage to elude Polito for the next two days. It's only until Wednesday, after all. The minute I step off that boat on Wednesday you can phone Inspector Santangelo at Organized Crime, tell him I'm out of the way, and send in the entire police department if you want."

"He'll be long gone by then," Crawley said, and Lieutenant Barker said, "I tend to agree with Jack."

"I'm sorry," said Levine, "but I don't. In the first place, he *won't* be long gone. I believe he actually will make it around the island tonight, but it won't be an easy trip. Those little boats always *feel* like they're going fast, but they're not. What's the top speed of a boat like that, on choppy open water? Twenty miles an hour, maybe a little more? And they gobble up gasoline, he'll have to stop once or twice at marinas. This rain will slow him down. Traveling as fast as he can, on a small boat pounding up and down over every wave, he'll be lucky if it only takes him seven or eight hours to get around to where he's supposed to meet me tomorrow."

Lieutenant Barker said, "Meaning what, Abe? How does that connect?"

"Meaning," Levine said, "he can't disappear from us all that easily."

Santangelo said, "That's not such good news, Abe. If *we* could find Banadando just like that, why can't Polito?"

Levine shrugged. "Maybe he can, I hope not. But we have the entire law enforcement apparatus behind us, to help, and Polito doesn't. We can bring in the Coast Guard, Army helicopters, anything we need."

Smiling, Santangelo said, "Not necessarily at the snap of our fingers."

"No, but it can be done. Polito can't begin to match our manpower or our authority."

Crawley said, "Never mind all of that after-the-event stuff,

Abe. What it comes down to is, Polito's people got to that pier today within an hour of *you* getting there. What if they'd been an hour earlier?"

"A lot of different things could have happened," Levine said.

"Some of them nasty," Crawley told him.

Santangelo said, "The decision has been Abe's from the beginning, and it still is. Abe, I'll go along with whatever you decide. But I have to say, there's a lot in what your partner says."

"I'll stay the course," Levine told him.

Santangelo said, "There's something else to consider. If something goes wrong, if Banadando gets killed or slips through our fingers, we could all be in trouble for not reporting the situation right away."

Levine spread his hands. "If you're worried about that, you do rank me after all, you could take the decision out of my hands."

"No, I don't want to," Santangelo said. "I think we're handling it right, but I want you and Fred and Officer Crawley to know there could be trouble for all of us down the line. Within the Department."

Lieutenant Barker said, "Let's count that out of the decision-making."

"Fine with me," Santangelo said.

The Long Island Expressway ended just short of Riverhead, seventy-five miles from Manhattan but still another forty-five miles from the end of the island at Montauk Point. The last dozen miles the traffic had thinned out so much that on the long straightaways Levine could see in the rearview mirror Jack Crawley's car, lagging way back. The rain had stopped sometime during the night but the sky was still cloud-covered and the air was cooler and still damp. In mid-morning, the sparse traffic here at the eastern end of the Expressway was mostly delivery vans and a few private cars containing shoppers, the latter mainly headed west toward the population centers.

The land out here seemed to imitate the wave-formations of the surrounding sea; long gradual rolls of scrub over which the highway moved in easy gradients, long sweeps steadily upward followed by long gradual declines. It was on the upslopes that Levine would catch glimpses of Jack Crawley's dark-green Pontiac far behind, and on the downslopes that he was increasingly alone.

At the Nugent Drive exit, two miles before the end of the highway, a car was entering the road, a black Chevrolet; Levine pulled accommodatingly into the left lane, passed the car, saw it recede in his mirror, and a moment later was over the next rise. Signs announced the end of the road.

The Chevy reappeared over the crest behind him so abruptly, moving so fast, that Levine had hardly time to register its presence in his mirror before it was shooting past him on the right and there were flat cracking sounds like someone breaking tree branches, and the wheel wrenched itself out of Levine's hands.

He'd been doing just over sixty. The Chevy was already far away in front, and Levine's car was slewing around toward the right shoulder, the wheel still spinning rightward. Levine grabbed it, fighting to pull it back to the left, his right foot tapping and tapping the brakes. Blow-out, he thought, but at the same time his mind was over-riding that normal thought, was telling him, No! They shot it out! They shot the tire!

Banadando! They found him, they're going after him! They cut me out of the play!

He was recapturing control, of his emotions and his thoughts and the car, when its right tires hit the gravel and dirt beside the road and tried to yank the steering wheel out of his hands again. He hung on, his foot tapping and tapping, pressing down harder as they slowed, daring to assert more and more control until at last, in a swirl of tan dust of its own creation, the car jolted to a stop, skewed slightly at an angle toward the highway, seeming to sag in exhaustion on its springs.

Levine opened his mouth wide to breath, but the constriction was farther back, deep in his throat. He leaned forward, resting his forehead on the top of the steering wheel, feeling its bottom press hard into his stomach. His trembling hand went up to cup his left ear, the position in which, he had learned, he could best hear his heart.

Beat, beat beat —
Skip.
Beat, beat, beat —
Skip.
Beat, beat, beat, beat —
Skip.
Beat, beat . . .

All right. Straightening, Levine took a deep breath, finding his throat more open, the act of breathing less painful. That had been a scary one.

Generally, the skips came every eighth beat, but excitement or exercise or terror could shorten the spaces. Three was about the closest it had ever come, and this near-accident had matched that record.

Accident? This was no accident. His entire body still slightly trembling, Levine struggled out of the car, walked around it, and saw that both right-side tires were flat. They showed garish big ragged holes in their sides. A sharp-shooter, worth the money Polito would be paying him.

Polito. Banadando. Feeling sudden urgency, Levine looked up the empty roadway toward the top of the slope he'd just come down. Crawley should have appeared by now, he wasn't that far back.

They've taken him out, too.

Jesus, what's happened to Crawley? Levine had actually trotted a few paces toward the distant crest when over it came a rattly white delivery van, and he remembered his other urgency instead: Banadando. In going for Levine's tires, Polito's men had made it clear they weren't interested in killing police today, so they'd undoubtedly taken out Jack Crawley the same way. The man in real trouble was Banadando.

Pulling his shield out of his jacket pocket, waving it in the air, Levine flagged the approaching van to a halt. A big boxy contraption advertising a brand of potato chip on its side, it was driven by a skinny bearded young man who stood up to drive. He was frowning at Levine with a kind of hopeful curiosity, as though here might be that which would rescue him from terminal boredom.

It was. The tall door on the right side of the van was hooked open. Climbing up into the tall vehicle, still showing the shield, Levine said, "Police. I'm commandeering this truck."

"*This* truck?" The young man grinned; shaking his head. "You got to be kidding."

"Drive," Levine told him. "As fast as this thing will go." To encourage the young man, he added, "We're trying to stop a murder."

"You're on, pal!"

But no matter how enthusiastic the young man might be, the van's top speed turned out to be just about fifty-two. Levine kept leaning his head out the open doorway, looking back, hoping to see Jack Crawley after all, but it never happened.

The interior of the van was piled high with outsize cardboard cartons, presumably containing potato chips. Levine leaned against the flat top of the dashboard under the high windshield and wrote a note on a sheet of paper torn from his memo pad:

"NYPD Detective Abraham Levine, 43 Precinct. Partner Jack Crawley in apparent accident on LIE. Underworld informant under attack. Follow caller to site."

After the highway ended, the young man followed

Levine's instructions along Old Country Road and Main Road and Church Lane and Sound Avenue. "It'll be a dirt road," Levine said. "On your left."

When they finally found it, the young man was going to swing to the left and drive down that road but Levine stopped him. Handing over the note, he said, "Go to the nearest phone, call the Suffolk County police, read this to them, tell them where I am."

"You might want me along," the young man said. "Maybe you could use some help."

"*Bring* me help," Levine told him. Stepping down to the shoulder of the road, he slapped the tinny side of the van as though it were a horse, calling to the driver, "Go on, now. Hurry!"

"Right!"

The van lumbered away, motor roaring as the young man tried to accelerate too rapidly up through the gears, and Levine trotted across the road and started down the dirt road, seeing the fresh scars and streaks of a car's having recently passed this way.

First he saw the water through the thin-leaved birch trees; Long Island Sound, separating this long tongue of land from Connecticut. Then he saw the automobile, a small fast low-to-the-ground Mercedes-Benz sports car painted dark blue. The black Chevy was nowhere in sight; Polito apparently employed specialists.

There was only the one car, and it contained seating for only two. Levine unlimbered his .38 S&W Police Special from its holster on his right hip and moved forward, stepping cautiously on the weedy leaf-covered ground. Yellow and orange leaves fluttered down, sometimes singly or when the breeze lifted they dropped in platoons, infiltrating their way to the ground.

Beyond the Mercedes muddy ground sloped down to an old wooden dock. Tied beside it, very close to shore, was the *Bobby's Dream*. Revolver in hand, eyes on the boat, Levine approached and, as he passed the Mercedes, a big-shouldered man in dark topcoat and hat came up out of the boat onto the dock, his arms full of boxes and packages, a couple of which Levine recognized; things he had brought to Banadando himself. He stopped, arm out, revolver aimed, and quietly said, "Just keep coming this way."

The man stopped, staring at Levine, his expression one of total amazement. Then, in a blindingly swift move, he flung the boxes away and his right hand stabbed within his topcoat.

Levine did not want to kill, but he did want to stop the man. He fired, aiming high on the man's torso on the right side, wanting to knock him down, knock him out of play, but still leave the breath of life in him. But the man was ducking, bobbing, just as Levine fired; when he jolted back, his own pistol flying out of his clothes and arcing away to fall into the water, Levine had no idea where he'd been hit. He went down hard, the sound a solid thud on the wooden boards of the dock, and he didn't move.

A sudden burst of pistol fire flared from the boat and Levine flung himself backward, putting the low bulk of the Mercedes between himself and the gunman. The firing stopped, and Levine sat on the leafy ground, revolver in his right hand, left hand pressed to his chest, mouth stretched wide. The constriction . . .

Hand cupped to ear. He counted beats, and after the fourth came the skip. Not too bad, not so bad as a little while ago in the car.

To his right, where he was sitting, were the hood and bumper and left front tire of the Mercedes, and out at an angle beyond them were the dock and the boat and the unmoving man Levine had shot. To his left, pressing against his arm, was the narrow graceful trunk of a birch tree. Levine sagged briefly against the tree, then pulled himself up onto his knees and looked cautiously over the hood.

Immediately the pistol cracked over there, and a fluttering of branches · took place somewhere behind Levine, who ducked back down. When nothing else happened, he called, "Banadando!"

"He don't feel like talking!" yelled a voice.

"Send him out here!"

"He don't feel like walking either!"

So he was dead already, which would give the man on the boat nothing to lose by holding out. Still, Levine called, "Come out of there with your hands up!"

"I'll tell him when he comes in!"

"You won't get away!"

"Yeah? Where's your army?"

"On its way," Levine called, but the constriction closed his throat again, chopping off the last word. Get here soon, he prayed.

The man on the boat swore loudly and fired twice in Levine's direction. Headlight glass shattered, and Levine couldn't help flinching away, his entire body clenching at each shot. "I'm comin' right through you!" yelled the voice.

"Come right ahead," Levine yelled. But he didn't yell it, he hoarsely coughed it. The tightness in his throat was making his head ache, was putting metal bands around his head just above his eyes. He *couldn't* pass out, he *had* to hold this fellow here. Bracing himself between the Mercedes and the tree trunk, he extended his arm forward onto the hood, where the revolver would be visible to the man in the boat. Hold him there. Hold him, no matter what.

Another shot pinged off the car's body; merely frustration and rage, but it made Levine wince. His free hand went to his ear, he sat looking at a leaf that had fallen into his lap.

Beat, beat, beat —

Skip.

Beat, beat —

Skip.

Beat, beat —

Skip.

Beat —

The Suffolk County cops were all over the dock, the boat, the foreshore. Boxes of Banadando's evidence were being carried to the cars. The gunman from the boat had already been taken away in handcuffs, and now they were waiting for the ambulance and the hearse.

Crawley stood with the Medical Examiner, who straightened and said, "He'd been dead at least a quarter hour when you got here."

"Yeah, I thought. And this one?"

They left Abe Levine's body and walked over to the wounded man on the dock, still unconscious but wrapped now in blankets from the police cars. "He'll live," the M.E. said.

"The wrong ones die," Crawley said.

"Everybody dies," the M.E. said. "It's a thing I've noticed."

Crawley turned and looked back at his partner. Abe was braced between the car and the tree, arm out straight, revolver just visible to the boat. He had died that way, his heart stopping forever but his body not moving. Sirens sounded, approaching.

"How do you like that," Crawley said. "He was dead, and he finished the job anyway. His corpse held that punk covered until we could get here."

"Maybe they'll give him a medal," the M.E. said, and grinned, showing uneven teeth. "A posthumous medal. The first legit posthumous medal ever, for performance above and beyond the call of death."

The hearse and ambulance were arriving. Crawley looked at the M.E. and pointed at Abe. "No plastic body bag," he said. "He gets a blanket."